Pageturners
35 Cambridge Road, Hove, BN3 1DE
www.pageturners.uk.com

First Edition January 2013

ISBN 10: 1482084007
ISBN 13: 9781482084009

Printed in the United Kingdom

Chapter One

I scrabble through my make-up bag, searching for some kind of magic remedy. There must be something in here which will make me look like a real actress.

My mind is racing on a million things at once. I have an audition in less than an hour with one of the biggest theatre companies in London. And although I graduated from England's best drama school this year, I majored in script writing. I have only ever acted in a handful of plays.

The lipstick skids out of my hand and falls to the floor. *Damn.* Maybe lipstick wasn't the look anyway. I turn back to face my reflection in the mirror.

Large, frightened grey eyes blink back at me from under a tangle of thick black hair. The best I can hope for is I get through the audition without making a complete fool of myself. I'll be lucky they don't laugh me out the door before I get to read my lines.

Lines. Another panic sets in. At least this I have prepared for. I begin muttering the learned words under my breath, like a mantra to calm my mind.

It doesn't work.

"Jeez, Issy. You look a wreck!"

Lorna, my best friend and housemate, breezes into my bedroom.

I say best friend. But since she was the one who swung this audition without asking me first, she is currently in my bad books.

"Lorna, they are going to take one look at me and burst out laughing," I frown, turning to face her. "It's obvious to anyone I'm not an actress."

Lorna stalks over to the bed, folding her long legs underneath herself as she sits. She's a model, and manages to make everything she does look like a catwalk pose.

"Shhh," she tuts, moving a tuft of hair out of my eyes. "Calm down. You'll be great. Remember the college play? You rocked the auditorium."

"That was at college, Lorna. This is the real thing."

Lorna cocks her head to one side and smiles. "We went to drama school, honey. They don't let anyone who isn't destined for greatness act in the final play. Besides, what have you got to lose?"

My dignity, my ego, my self-respect.

I look back to the mirror, letting out a long sigh.

Lorna shrugs. "I couldn't have even got you this audition if you hadn't shown talent. Berkeley Theatre only lets top actors try out for their plays."

The thought spikes me with a fresh surge of fear.

Top actors. And me. Great.

"And you're perfect for the role," continues Lorna. "Look at your beautiful dark hair and those great big eyes. You're a natural Lady Capulet."

This is another reason why I'm annoyed with Lorna. She chose the role without asking me. And yet again, I've been typecast as an evil older woman.

I give my reflection a rueful smile. *Thanks mom.* In the few roles I've acted, my inherited Spanish features always get me cast as villainesses and femme fatales. Ironic, since nothing else about me suits those roles. I've only had two boyfriends and one of those was in first grade.

"Just think, if you get it," continued Lorna, her eyes shining, "you could get to meet James Berkeley in person. Or even Madison Ellis!"

I frown into the mirror. Right now, meeting the famous owner of the Berkeley Theatre company and his actress wife is the last thing on my mind. All I want to do is get through the audition without mangling my lines too badly and leave with my dignity.

"I just have no idea how I should look," I sigh. "I never went to those classes about how to ace auditions."

"Turn to face me," instructs Lorna. I obey, and she riffles through my make-up until she has a stack of neutral shades in her palm.

"It's just like casting for models," she says. "You just have to look like you're not trying too hard and that you're naturally beautiful. Which for you," she adds, sticking an eye pencil between her teeth, "issh the eashieest sshing in the world."

I sit still whilst Lorna applies neutral tones of brown and taupe around my pale grey eyes.

"I'm sorry," I say as she gets to work on my face. "I am grateful, Lorna. Truly. It's just that I think I'm way out of my league here."

Lorna acknowledges the apology and switches to a different make-up brush. Under her expert hands, my eyes now appear both professionally finished and effortlessly natural.

"Thanks," I say, admiring her genius with make-up.

"Phew," says Lorna, smudging away at the final layer. "This is tougher than it looks. Even the slightest dash of pencil is going to make you look like a smouldering sex kitten. *Not* the look," she adds, leaning back to appraise my face.

"Ok," she concludes, "I think we're going to have to do without mascara. Your eyelashes are so long, they might end up looking false."

"Lorna!" I laugh. I love my friend but her flattery is beyond ridiculous sometimes. It must be her life in the modelling world.

I look at the pair of us in the mirror. Without a lick of make-up, Lorna's chocolate skin has a perfect golden sheen to it. She looks like she's been airbrushed, and her violet eyes sing out against her tumult of afro hair. Everything about Lorna is vivacious. Full of life. She has got every single modelling job she has ever tried for, and London agents are falling over themselves to represent her. Next to Lorna, I look like a ghost.

"It should be you going to the audition," I murmur, gazing at her beautiful face. "Not me."

Lorna turns to me sternly.

"Now you listen to me, Isabella Green," she admonishes, waving a long finger. "You are a superbly talented young actress.

And you're perfect for this role. Don't you dare waste this opportunity."

I smile back at her. "I'll do my very best," I say. "I promise." And I mean it. Lorna's gone out of her way to land me this chance. The least I can do is put my all into it.

"Besides," Lorna looks puzzled for a moment. "I thought you wanted to try out acting."

"I did," I sigh. "But for some small, independent theatre company. Somewhere I could be involved in the scripts. I never wanted to try with the biggest theatre company in the country. And for Romeo and Juliet of all the plays!"

The realisation of what Lorna's put me up for is starting to hit hard. It's true that I do want to try some acting in a small way. But not as the centre of attention in some big production. I never saw my name in lights like the other kids at drama school. My place is behind the scenes, in the background. I only want to act a little so I can be a better script writer.

"Well, there's no harm in hitting the big time too early. And you owe me." Lorna gives me an evil grin. "I had to sleep with the choreographer to get you this audition."

"You didn't!" For a moment, I think she's serious. Lorna nearly falls off the bed laughing.

"Of course not! Honey, I'm bad but I'm not that bad. I told you before. We met at a party. I mentioned your name. He'd caught the last of the college final play and thought you'd be good."

"Ok." I stand. "Clothes." My heartbeat starts hammering again.

Lorna selects a pair of tight designer jeans, which she insisted I buy in the summer sales, and then runs off to find me a top from her bedroom.

"Here," she returns, holding a beautiful silk camisole top.

"I can't wear that!" I yelp. The top probably costs more than my waitressing salary earns me in a month.

"Take it, take it," Lorna waves it at me.

"It looks like underwear," I say dubiously, taking the top.

"That's the look this season," says Lorna. "They'll think you're beautiful *and* have your finger on the fashion pulse. What's not to love?"

"Ok." I take a deep, panic-wracked breath as I slide on the silky top. As an afterthought, I grab my favourite black vintage suit jacket and slip it over the top. Lorna nods in approval.

"You look great," she says. "You always could mix in the vintage thing."

"I'm good to go," I say, appraising the new 'casual-audition-Isabella' in the mirror.

Lorna sits on the bed. She looks a little tired suddenly.

"Did you remember to take your tablets?" I say, suddenly remembering that she came in late last night.

Lorna has been a diabetic since childhood, but unless I watch her like a hawk, she sometimes forgets to take her meds.

"Of course! Stop worrying about me and concentrate on the audition," says Lorna.

She stands and gives me a hug. "You go," she says. "Have fun. You look perfect. Really great. Don't do anything I wouldn't do. And if you see that hot Mr James Berkeley, you blow him a little kiss from me."

I laugh and feel my heartbeat slow just a little. "As if I would! Anyway, Berkeley is only a financial investor, Lorna. He doesn't get involved in the production side. The theatre would be lucky if he even showed up to a premiere."

"Well," says Lorna, "you never know. You might get the part, and then you'll see him at that premiere when he shows up."

Chapter 2

I emerge from the London underground in the bustle of Covent Garden. Ordinarily, I come here with Lorna shopping. And a couple of times we've managed to get cheap theatre tickets to West End shows. But I've never come here with a real schedule, and the tangle of London streets are confusing.

Nervously, I consult my home-made map. As usual, I printed it last minute, only to discover my ancient Epson was running low on ink. Again. The London streets on the map are only half-printed and the result is difficult to read.

I realise that one of the huge redbrick Victorian buildings looks familiar.

Have I walked down this street already?

I check my watch. *Damn.* The last thing I need is to be the girl who turns up late.

It must be here somewhere.

I stare up at the billboards peppering the historic buildings. There are at least ten theatres on this street and it's hard to tell where one ends and the next begins.

I check my map again and look up at a vast façade of ornate stonework.

My heart rises into my throat. This is the right building, and I remember where I've seen it before.

One night, when Lorna dragged me to a West End bar, we went past this theatre, and the streets were clogged with people queuing for miles back to get in. Then three huge black limos pulled up and the crowd went crazy.

"That's the royal entourage," said Lorna knowledgably, pointing to a discreet gold crest on one of the doors. "Looks like Princes William and Harry are making a visit to the theatre."

At the time, we'd both stood and stared, trying to get a glimpse of the princes. I never imagined I'd have a reason to go inside.

But here I am. About to audition at a theatre which is the choice of the British Royal Family. And on Lorna's advice, I've opted for dress-down jeans and a camisole top.

I approach the plush-looking doors, swallowing hard.

An immaculately-suited doorman complete with top hat steps neatly forward and opens the door for me.

I step through. The world on the other side is so much more fabulous than I'm used to that it takes my breath away.

Beneath my feet, the plush red carpet feels a mile deep, whilst the elaborate ceilings soar into a wealth of glittering chandeliers and gold-leaf. The walls are decked with images of famous actors, and in between it all is the dark mahogany of the ticket office and the information service.

Anxiously, I approach the ticket office, feeling my muscles tighten with nerves.

A young woman in gold and green liveried suit looks up. Her lipstick is so perfect, it makes her mouth look like a magazine cover shot.

"Can I help you?" she smiles. I blink, momentarily overwhelmed by her flawless make-up. Surely she must have someone do it for her?

"I'm here to audition," I say, adding, "Lorna Hamilton arranged it."

The woman's face twists in confusion.

"They sent you up here?" she says. "You usually need to go to the stage door."

Of course I should have gone to the stage door! It's as much as I can do not to slap my hand against my forehead. *What a complete idiot to think I could just walk into the main theatre.*

"It's back outside and round the corner," she adds, kindly catering to my obvious idiocy.

I nod. "Thanks. Um. Thank you."

"They probably haven't put the right signs up," adds the woman. "It's absolute chaos today." She lowers her voice conspiratorially. "James Berkeley has flown in from LA unannounced, and everyone is running around like a headless chicken!"

"I… I thought he was only a financer," I say, curiosity getting the better of me. James Berkeley *is* James Berkeley after all. In the movie world, he is one of the biggest directors and producers out there. Not to mention he is seriously hot.

The woman smiles, obviously sharing my interest.

"Usually, he doesn't get involved. But he's interested in nurturing young talent. So sometimes he flies in to see how the rehearsals are going. It's a real honour for the actors," she adds.

I give a half smile in reply before turning on my heel and heading the way I've just come.

It surprises me that the woman speaks so warmly of Berkeley. In the movie world, he's known for his take-no-prisoners approach to filming and has a reputation for working staff to the brink of exhaustion. Maybe he has a different approach to theatre.

I make my way out of the plush doors and eventually find the considerably less glamorous stage door round the back of the theatre.

Maybe James Berkeley arriving is a blessing in disguise, I think. Perhaps everyone will be too distracted to notice I'm a few minutes late.

I knock and, after a moment, someone buzzes me in. I enter and am confronted with a grouchy-looking woman behind a glass panel. She must be in her mid-fifties and looks as though she's been here since the theatre was built.

"I… Um… I'm here for an audition," I manage.

She glowers at me and looks at her watch meaningfully.

The clock behind her head reads a few minutes past the hour.

"I'm sorry I'm late," I add. "I went to the wrong place."

The woman raises her eyebrows.

"Name?"

"Isabella Green." She consults her list for what feels like an age. Then, just when I think she's going to find a reason to send me away, she points a coral-painted fingernail along the dark corridor.

"That way," she says. "Third door left."

I nod gratefully. She leans forward.

"Do. Not," she says, pronouncing every word, "go running around into different rooms. Mr Berkeley is here to watch the rehearsals today, and the last thing he needs is some love-struck young performer interrupting him."

As if I would blow my audition to go act the dumb fan! I am outraged. James Berkeley may be a famous director, but I'm not about to go running around trying to catch a glimpse of him.

Temper, temper. Keep yourself in check.

I bite back a tart reply, reminding myself to keep my hot-headedness under control.

I've learned the hard way that having my mother's Spanish temperament can be less than helpful in professional situations.

So I choose to ignore the comment and turn away from her, stalking off down the corridor.

I'm still letting the annoyance subside as I find the door marked 'auditions'. I take a moment outside to steel myself.

Lorna has told me all about the casting director. She's a formidable woman and unforgiving of slip-ups. I feel the nerves begin to build again.

I've learned all my lines, I remind myself. *At least she can't be angry at me for that.*

Slightly calmer, I raise my hand and knock on the door.

"Come in!"

To my surprise, it's not a female voice but a male who calls from inside.

Perhaps she has an assistant. Or a bevy of other people in to help her watch the casting. I don't know how big theatres work, but this makes sense.

I push down the handle and walk in.

But in the room there is only one person. And as the familiar face turns to me, I feel my heart drop into my shoes.

I can't believe it.

James Berkeley himself is conducting the audition.

Chapter 3

For a long moment my feet won't move forward, and it's all I can do to keep my mouth dropping open in amazement.

Then my resolve kicks in and I force my legs to move across the room.

The audition space is small, with just a single chair in which Berkeley sits and a mock stage taped-out in white tape.

Easy, Isabella, I say to myself. *Just one step at a time.*

I have no idea how I'm going to get my lines out.

I take in the taped-out stage area. It's about fifteen foot square. Bigger than I was expecting. Somewhere in my panic-frozen brain, I mentally scale up some of my acted movements to fill the area.

"You're late," says Berkeley as I approach the taped-out area in front of his director's chair.

"And you're not who I was expecting," I mutter. My rising fear is mixing with a feeling of aggravation. What a stunt to pull! Surely even a seasoned professional would be intimidated to find a world-famous director conducting their audition instead of the usual casting director.

Or perhaps this is just a mean trick to weed out the less experienced actors. In my case, it's bound to work.

"You are not who I was expecting either," he says in a low voice. The way he speaks seems to have an extra resonance, and his words rumble around the small room.

My legs manage to carry me into the designated acting area. Berkeley stares into my face as I stand in the acting area and turn to him. We are about six feet apart, but for some reason, the distance feels a lot closer. The atmosphere is almost intimate. I feel my cheeks begin to heat and pray I'm not blushing.

He's dressed plainly in the classic director's black jeans and T-shirt. I've seen this look a hundred times in drama school. But clinging to his broad chest and muscular thighs, they take on a new level of sexy.

He's so hot. The thought leaps into my head, unbidden.

There's a rustle of paper as he consults his notes.

"Isabella Green?" he says. The corner of his mouth twitches, just fractionally.

"Yes."

"And you are auditioning for Lady Capulet?" He sounds confused.

I let out a breath.

"Yes."

"I apologise for the last minute change in who you were expecting. Nancy has been called away," he says, his tone explanatory.

The words compute in my brain. *Nancy. Nancy Mendes. The casting director. He's explaining why he's here instead of her.*

"She's having some… personal problems, and so I offered to step in," he adds. "Nancy is a good friend of mine."

She must be a very good friend if he flew here all the way from LA. I wonder idly what his wife must think of her famous husband jetting halfway across the world to help out a female friend.

"You know who I am?" he asks.

His accent is aristocratic English, I realise – something I hadn't noticed in the nerves of my first arrival. He speaks in the definite tones of the British upper class.

I nod, fractionally. *Of course I know who you are!* my brain screams.

Every drama student knows about the famous producer-director and his equally famous actress wife.

"Your first film became a cult classic," I mumble, consulting my student knowledge bank, "and it made you the youngest director to win an Oscar for Best Picture. Then your next three films became huge box office hits."

He gives a slight smile, as if amused to see his work summarised.

"Quite so. Thank you for the biography," he agrees in clipped tones, and I can't tell if he's flattered or horrified by my childish description of his career. But something about the tone of his answer goads me.

"You're also notorious for pushing actors to their limits," I retort, "and the rumour is that you're known as 'the hammer' on-set for your work-all-hours approach."

I regret the words almost as soon as they are out of my mouth. *Damn my Spanish hot-headedness. Will I ever learn?*

Berkeley's eyebrows raise and my sudden rush of courage deserts me.

I stare at him nervously, trying to gauge the effect of my last remark. He seems completely unconcerned.

"The actors who complain of the work do not complain when they win awards," he says without emotion.

It's as much as I can do to concentrate on why I'm here, and I realise I'm staring at his mouth. I've seen James Berkeley in magazines. Everyone has. But in real life, the seductive charm he oozes in photographs is dialled up to the next level.

"I didn't realise you had such an interest in theatre," I stumble, filling the silence with the first thing which comes into my head.

He looks surprised.

"I have an interest in all dramatic arts," he says. "Some of my interests are more financial than hands-on. But that doesn't mean I don't find the time to be personally involved when my movie schedule allows."

He sounds annoyed.

Great start Isabella.

"Well then," he says, his accent rounding off every word. "You'd better show me what you can do."

Something about the way he says it suggests he finds the idea funny.

He can already see I shouldn't be here. The thought brings a white surge of panic to my stomach and I fight to push it down.

Get out the lines, do your best, and get out of here, I say to myself. It's the best I can hope for.

I walk to the centre of the stage. My script is in my hand because that's what's expected at an audition. But I don't need it. I've learned everything by heart.

The part I've rehearsed is Lady Capulet's biggest scene. Where she tells Juliet she must marry a man she doesn't love.

I close my mind for a moment and try to let the character flow.

Then I take a deep breath and begin. But I've only uttered a few lines when Berkeley stops me.

"You're not using your script," he says.

I swing to face him, totally wrong-footed in the middle of my performance.

"I. Um. I've learned it by heart," I say.

He gives a sardonic smile. "How very diligent."

Great. So James Berkeley doesn't like me. He could at least have the manners to let me finish my performance.

Trying not to let his disapproval put me off, I carry on for a few more lines. But after a moment, he interrupts again.

"What do you think Lady Capulet is feeling at this moment?" he asks.

I stare at him in confusion. But this, at least, is something I can answer.

"She thinks her domineering husband might do something terrible to Juliet," I say. "She loves her daughter. But she realises that it is best for Juliet if she marries Paris instead of Romeo."

"You don't think that Lady Capulet has her own selfish motives?"

The script in my hand is shaking a little, but I still myself.

"No," I say, defending my own reading of the play. "That's not how I read it. I think she's doing the best to protect her daughter in a difficult situation."

"I see." His voice is crisp, and I realise I have blown it. *This must be what the life of an actor is like*, I think grimly. I should have known it wasn't for me. The rejection comes like a sharp jab in the pit of my stomach.

"What made you decide to audition as Lady Capulet?" he asks, more kindly now. I realise he's breaking the news that I'm not right for the part.

"My friend Lorna put me forward," I admit.

I have nothing to lose now, so I might as well tell the truth. It's obvious I have no right to be here anyway. "She chose the role," I add.

Berkeley frowns.

I lower my script and stare at the ground.

"Thank you for your consideration," I say. To my embarrassment, the words come out choked. There are tears in my eyes.

"Wait." The authority in his voice echoes around the small room and stops me in my tracks as I make to leave the stage area.

Berkeley is on his feet. He moves towards me, and suddenly there are two players on the stage. James Berkeley and me.

Whoa. It's almost too much to take in.

He is so close, I can smell his cologne. It is a musky, heady smell. I have to stop myself consciously breathing him in.

"I liked your reading of Lady Capulet," he says. "You brought a dimension to her I hadn't seen before."

I feel a flush of pleasure. *He liked my performance.* Then reality kicks in. *Get a hold of yourself, Isabella. That doesn't mean he wants to cast a nobody.*

Up close, I can see his features in far greater detail. Photographs in the press have not done him justice. His features are perfect, as though he has been sketched by an artist. But they have just the slightest unevenness about them, giving him a roguish look. The combination is heart-stoppingly sexy.

"Let me read with you," he says, stepping a little closer.

I realise I am holding my breath. He must know the effect he has on women. I am staring at his mouth again and flick my eyes away. The knowledge brings with it a slow blush, and I try to pick a non-sexual feature to focus on.

But wherever my gaze rests brings a new part of his perfect face into detail. Deep green eyes. Heavy eyebrows. Chiselled cheekbones. I settle on the space above his sculpted nose and prey the blush isn't as obvious as it feels.

"I think you are miscast as Lady Capulet," he says. He is staring at me intently. "Do you know Juliet's lines in this scene?"

I nod dumbly. Of course. I learned both roles. You need to do that to understand the character.

Berkeley nods. He seems impressed. "Quite the professional you are," he says.

I flush again. He's mocking me.

"Well then," he says, "let's see whether you understand an innocent Juliet as well as you play the misunderstood Lady Capulet."

Juliet! I've never played a main character.

"I'm not sure I'm ready for Juliet," I mumble. "I've never played a main role."

I raise my eyes to meet his, and as I catch his dark expression, I look quickly back to the floor. "I've only played bit parts," I add, wincing at the confession. Surely he'll throw me out now? What kind of person turns up to an audition at a major theatre having never played a main role?

"You're not ready for Juliet?" he murmurs. I hear amusement in his voice, but I can't bring myself to look up off the floor.

"But is Juliet ready for you?" he says.

This confuses me enough to raise my gaze, and I see a part-smile lighting his features in a devilish cast.

"You will read Juliet," he snaps, his voice suddenly drained of humour. "And I will read Lord Capulet."

This must be what it's like to work with James Berkeley, I think, wincing at the severity of his tone.

I look down at the script distractedly. And suddenly his fingers close around it.

"Let's do without these, shall we?" he says, tugging the script free from my hands. "Better we go naked, since you've learned the part."

It's a theatre term I've heard hundreds of times. It means acting without a script. But for some reason, when he says it, it has a different meaning. I have a sudden image of us both naked on the stage. I wonder what he looks like beneath his black director's jeans and T-shirt. I blush crimson.

Berkeley drops both scripts on the floor.

"I know every line in Romeo and Juliet," he says in answer to my unspoken question. "We shall begin on line 2225."

I glance at the script.

2225. Juliet. My line.

I've spoken these words before, in my bedroom, and tried to imagine what it must feel like to be Juliet – hopelessly in love but forced to marry where she doesn't love. I open my mouth and the words come out.

"Not proud you have, but thankful," I begin, staring up into his face.

It's hard not to look away, but I hold his gaze. "But I beseech you, I can never marry where I hate."

The words bring with them the character, and I gratefully tumble into the role of Juliet, letting the theatre and James Berkeley melt into the play.

"You shall marry Paris," says Berkeley, and the anger in his voice comes off him in waves.

Holy hell. He can really act.

I have never read lines with someone so accomplished before. His anger seems so real, it scares me deeper into character.

I drop to my knees for the next line, staring up at him. His fury feels overwhelming, and I am begging it to subside.

"Sir," I say, "I beseech you on my knees."

Something else is in his eyes now. Am I imagining it?

He looks like he wants to devour me.

"You are mine," he growls, "and as mine I give you to my friend. And if you are not mine, I leave you to starve and beg in the streets."

As he speaks the words I feel something stir within me. My body feels hot and my breath is tight in my chest. Is this what they mean by chemistry on stage?

"Is there no pity in you, Sir?" I plead, my voice thick with desperation. I stand and, swept up in the act, I place my hands flat on his chest in a gesture of supplication. The contact brings with it an electric shock, and suddenly I am Isabella again, staring up at his hard green eyes.

For a second, he too seems to have broken character and is gazing into my face. Then the anger loads back into his features.

I swallow and Juliet returns. "That sees the bottom of my grief?" I conclude, taking away my hands and moving them to cover my mouth.

Instead of answering, Berkeley turns and makes a few paces away from me. He seems to be lost in his own thoughts, and I realise the act is over.

My body is only just catching up with my mind. It's swirling with a depth of emotion that I've never felt before. The proximity to Berkeley was overwhelming, and even though he's only stepped a few feet away, I feel as though I've been severed.

Then the waves of disappointment begin to wash over me. He stopped the scene so quickly. I wasn't good enough then, after all.

"That was very interesting," he says finally, as though reading my thoughts.

Interesting. Great.

I stand awkwardly, embarrassment flooding back now that I'm Isabella again, alone in a theatre with James Berkeley.

He turns to me. "There is something about your acting," he says, and then he stops.

I stare dumbly back at him, wondering what he means.

"I usually find people easy to read, easy to place," he mutters, staring at me. "But you. You are a mystery. I have no idea what character might bring out the best in you."

He looks genuinely distressed, and I wonder if this is some artist insecurity. But somehow I don't think so. I can't imagine James Berkeley is ever usually uncertain.

"We have already cast Juliet to a known actress," he says, "and I am not sure that would be your part in any case."

In a sudden movement, he is back in his chair, looking at his watch.

"I've let this audition overrun," he says. "Not something I have ever done before," he adds, almost to himself.

I realise he is dismissing me.

"Thank you for your consideration," I say, picking the script up off the floor. I make to hand it back to him as I leave, but he gestures I should keep it.

"The casting decision is not made for six months," he says. "You will hear whether you were successful then."

I nod and walk out of the audition room, finally making sense of what's just happened.

I've had an audition with James Berkeley. He was generous enough to try me out for a different kind of role in the play. And I disappointed him after a few lines.

The thought is so unexpectedly painful that a few tears come to my eyes.

I hastily brush them away, furious with myself.

Toughen up, Isabella, I growl at myself as I leave the theatre. *You wanted to try your luck at acting. You just got what you deserved.*

Chapter 4

I make my way home on the underground in a daze. *James Berkeley. And he said he liked my acting.*

This, at least, brings a little surge of glee to salve the disappointment of messing up the audition.

I get off the underground in Chelsea, the London district where Lorna and I share an apartment. My phone beeps in my pocket. I've missed three calls from my mother since I've been travelling under London's busy streets.

I press to return the call, and just as I think she's not going to pick up, the phone answers.

"Darling!" My mother's Spanish accent sounds warm.

"Hello, Mami."

"Darling, I had a feeling something might be wrong."

"No, Mami. I had the audition I told you about." This is typical of my mother. She has a sixth sense for when I'm in emotional turmoil.

"How exciting, darling! When will you hear back?"

"Six months."

My mother ponders this. "That is a long time. Did you do well?"

"I don't think so. The producer was doing the casting. It was intimidating."

"Oh darling, I will never know why you think so little of yourself. I am sure you were magnificent, *carina.*"

I smile. *Carina* is Spanish for *darling*, and my mother uses it often.

"How are you doing for money, Isabella?"

"Fine. I still have the waitressing job. It's good enough money."

I hear a deep sigh at the end of the line.

"I am so sorry, Isabella. When your father left you his apartment in Chelsea, he wanted it to be a blessing. And now it is a curse because of these legal vultures."

I am laughing a little. "Don't be so dramatic, Mami."

"I will never understand it," she continues. I can almost see her brows knitting on the other end of the phone. "Why is it so complicated?"

"It's not that complicated, Mami," I sigh. "Dad left the apartment to me when he died. But the building comes with a service charge to cover the upkeep of the building."

"But why is it so much, *carina*? It is thousands of pounds."

"Mami, I've told you this a hundred times. Chelsea is a really expensive part of London. People who live here are millionaires. They expect to pay a lot in service charges."

The annual fee is so high that Lorna and I wind up paying the same in service charges as we would renting in another part of the city. But we have a much nicer apartment, and the location is perfect for Lorna's modelling work and West End theatres.

"I promise I will manage the legal things," says my mother.

I have heard this before. If she could bring herself to deal with the lawyers, the apartment can be negotiated service-free. But my mother never could stomach legal papers.

"I do it this month," she promises. I know she won't, and I don't have the heart to force the issue.

"Ok, Mami," I say, "but it's fine really. The service charge is the same as rent," I repeat, "and we're the only drama graduates I know who have a doorman in a fancy hat."

My mother laughs.

"Ok, darling," she says. "Listen, I'm going to come to London to visit you in a few days. I go now. You take care. I love you."

"Ok. See you soon then. Love you too, Mami."

I hang-up, mentally tidying the flat of Lorna's clothes for my mother's visit. My early childhood was spent travelling in a VW with my parents' puppet show, and my mother is the last person to care about a little mess. But I always like to make sure the apartment is nice for when she comes.

I'm at the door of my apartment block now, and Peter, the doorman, opens the door. I smile. Peter has been doing this job for twenty years, and we often share a joke. He knows I'm the only person in the entire block besides Lorna who doesn't have a Porsche and a trust fund.

But today, I'm too distracted by the audition to do much more than say hello and take the hundred-year old elevator to my floor.

As soon as my key hits the door, I hear Lorna open it from the other side, and I'm greeted by her brightly-lit features.

"Soooo…. How'd it go?" She is beyond excited. I manage a weak smile.

"James Berkeley was filling in for the casting director."

Her face makes a comical round of confusion until she finally figures I'm not joking.

"Seriously?" she manages. Her voice comes out as a squeak. She's lusted after James Berkeley since forever.

"Yes." I give her a rueful smile and walk through the hallway into the lounge. Lorna follows after and I flop onto the sofa.

"It was kinda off putting," I say.

Lorna laughs. "I bet! What was he like? Up close? Was he as handsome as he looks in the pictures?"

I smile. "More," I say. "Much more."

Lorna gasps suddenly and claps her hands over her mouth.

"Oh my God!" she screams. "Isabella Green! You're hot for him! I can see it!"

I feel my features start to burn.

"Don't be stupid, Lorna," I mutter. "He's a married man."

"Since when did marriage matter to lust?" She's peering at me intently, as though trying to figure something out.

"Did he make a pass at you?"

"Of course not!"

Lorna shrugs. "Wouldn't surprise me. It would be him and every other man on the planet."

I shake my head. For Lorna, my love life is complicated by its non-existence. I've had a few experiences at college, and I'm no virgin at least. But I've never really found anyone who I felt anything much for other than friendship.

With a sudden jolt of shock, I remember the chemistry I felt on stage with Berkeley.

Maybe that's what it's all about.

I quickly dismiss the thought.

"Well anyway," Lorna is saying as I try to school my unruly mind, "you might see him again tonight."

"What?"

What!

"Ha," says Lorna, "that got your attention."

She's totally right.

See him again tonight? How? I am horrified to realise I am excited about the idea. *What happened to morality, Green? He's married.*

"From a distance anyway," concedes Lorna.

Oh. My heartbeat returns to something fractionally more like normal.

"Because…" Lorna pauses, ever the drama queen, to make the big reveal. "I've got us invites to the launch tonight at Mahiki!"

"Mahiki?" I say the word uncertainly. London's most famous club is the favourite late night hang-out of the two royal princes, as well as London's richest and most famous people.

Even I have heard about the launch there tonight. It's for a new film which is already building huge critical acclaim. It makes sense that James Berkeley would attend, since he's in London. But he'll be sectioned off in a VIP area like all the other super-celebrities. Whilst wannabes like me and Lorna are squished in with the B list – not an unpleasant thought for someone like Lorna. But I've never been a huge fan of loud nights out on the celebrity circuit.

Lorna senses my uncertainty.

"Oh, there is NO way you're not going," she announces. "I need your pretty face to get us to the front of the queue. The two of us will be impossible to refuse."

She grins. "Come on, Isabella. Don't tell me you're thinking of staying home."

I am. Staying home and trying to sort out the mess of thoughts and feelings caused by today's audition.

But Lorna got me the audition and she's my best friend.

I sigh. "Ok, fine."

Lorna bounces on the couch.

"Ok!" She checks her watch. "Then we'd better start getting ready. Only a few hours until the doors open, and we need to look our best."

Chapter 5

Lorna insists I dial-up my usual vintage look to something sexier. So we both arrive at Mahiki's glittering doors clad in the latest fashion.

She's dug me out a dress which was gifted her by a designer. It's silver, with geometric slashes of lime and purple at the hips and shoulder straps.

The dress only comes to mid-thigh, which is higher than I'm used to. Particularly since my feet are clad in a pair of fake Jimmy Choo copies which are three inches higher than my usual heel height.

Lorna wears skin-tight jeans and cowboy boots teamed with a top which barely covers her nipples. It's held in place with artfully placed tape and shows off flashes of her glowing coffee-coloured back and stomach.

"Better than mortal man deserves." Lorna grins at me as we head arm in arm for the entrance.

Like most of the exclusive London clubs, the doorway is tiny, understated, with only a small gold sign announcing this is the legendary Mahiki.

But the club doesn't need a sign with people stretched around the block to get in.

"Come on," says Lorna, heading for the front. I tug against her arm.

"Lorna," I hiss, "there's a line!"

"Not for us," she says, and heads straight for the doorman.

I'm hoping the ground will open up and swallow us as she drags past the evil glares of the queue.

The doorman recognises her instantly, and the expression on his face changes from hostile to a broad smile.

"Hello pretty lady," he says.

Lorna returns the smile. I wonder how they know each other. You'd swear they were best friends.

"Go right in," the doorman adds, letting us ease past the tight queue of people.

"That's not fair, Lorna," I protest as we follow the soft red carpet along the entrance hall. "All those people have to wait in the cold!"

Lorna shrugs. "Their choice," she says unrepentantly. "If they want to come to this club, they have to wait. If they don't want to wait, they should be younger, prettier or richer."

I roll my eyes.

"Come on," says Lorna, "let's get to the bar."

It's the first time I've been inside Mahiki, and the experience is like an explosion of gold and red. It reminds me of Aladdin's cave teamed with a pirate ship. The bar is decked out to look like the world's most glamorous beach bar, with wicker chairs and bamboo pillars.

Gorgeous barmen whisk up cocktails with Champagne and spirits at lightning speed, and all the drinkers are young and beautiful.

"Look!" I squeak, pointing to a familiar face, "is that who I think it is?"

Lorna nods, looking towards the supermodel. "She doesn't come here very often anymore. She prefers the Met Bar. But I guess she's made an exception for the launch. Come on," she adds, scouting the bar area, "let's find a good place to stand."

But as we head for the bar, we're interrupted.

"Can I buy you ladies a drink?" asks a handsome brown-haired man, gazing first at me and then at Lorna. He's in his mid-twenties, and dressed in the kind of clothes that appear artfully casual but cost more than a Saville Row suit.

Lorna is at her charming best. She bats her long false lashes and gives him a killer smile.

"That depends who's asking," she says.

He smiles back and puts his hand out.

"Ben Gracey," he says.

Lorna's eyes widen. "As in *the* Ben Gracey?"

"My father is *the* Gracey," he says modestly. "I'm only due to inherit. Does that mean I get to buy you a drink?" he adds, looking at both of us.

"Hell yes," says Lorna. "Landed gentry passes the test. I'll have a Champagne cocktail."

"Lorna!" I say, thinking of her diabetes.

"I'll be fine," she dismisses my concern with a hand-wave. "It's only one drink."

"And for you?" Ben is looking intently into my face.

"Nothing for me," I say.

"Are you sure?" Ben insists. "It's no trouble."

"Um. Ok, I'll have a lime and soda," I say, feeling a little guilty. Usually I prefer to buy my own drinks, but my monthly wage doesn't stretch to Mahiki prices. I was planning on sticking to water.

He frowns. "Wouldn't you rather something stronger? I'm buying."

I shake my head. "No thanks."

"Are you sure?" he presses. "Maybe a little vodka with the soda?"

I shake my head again, and Lorna, ever my saviour, steps in.

"She doesn't drink. Don't make a big deal of it," she says. "She had a bad experience in a bar a few years ago."

It was more than bad. I remember the hands gripping at me and shake the memory away.

"Oh," Ben looks embarrassed. "Ok, well, Champagne cocktail. Lime soda. I'll be right back."

"Lorna!" I hiss as he heads to the bar. "You don't have to tell everyone my life story."

"What?" Lorna is staring distractedly after Ben. "Oh, I'm sorry honey. It just slipped out. In the future, I'll tell everyone you're a model and you're watching your skin, ok?"

"Just say I don't drink," I mutter, thinking that would be worse. I pray that Ben won't remember and start asking me about the "bad experience". I hate having to avoid questions.

"He's got access to the VIP area," observes Lorna, watching Ben move across the crowded bar. I look to see him enter a zone of low-lit tables where the clientele are invisible. They are surrounded by burly-looking men who I assume must be bodyguards.

"But not the super VIP," she observes as he avoids a huddle of low-lit banquets guarded by immaculate club-hired bouncers.

"Super VIP?" This is news to me.

"Sure," confirms Lorna with a nod. "On big nights like this, Mahiki put on another tier of importance. Even the regular celebs can't get into the Gold Zone. That's strictly for Hollywood royalty."

She stares at the area longingly. "What I would give to take a peek in there," she says wistfully.

Ben returns, handing Lorna a crystal flute filled with glittering Champagne and topped with gold leaf.

His drink is a dark red cocktail in a long glass, and in his other hand is a straight glass of lime-soda, which he hands to me.

"Thanks." I take a grateful sip. The sparkling lime is super-refreshing.

"So what brings you ladies to Mahiki?" asks Ben, raising his glass in a toast. For some reason, there is something in his eyes I don't quite trust. I tug my skirt down and I see his gaze flick down to follow the gesture.

"Gorgeous men," says Lorna, meeting his eyes. He laughs, not unnerved by Lorna's no-nonsense approach.

"I'm a model," she adds, by way of explanation, "and my friend is an actress. We went to drama school together."

"An actress?" he turns to me in interest. "Were you in the film?"

I blush, realising he's talking about the film this launch party is all about.

"No. I'm only just starting out," I say. "I'm not much of an actress."

"She aced the graduation play, and a critic from *The Times* said she was the best new talent he'd ever seen," interrupted Lorna, ever eager to show off my attributes. "And she had an audition today with James Berkeley."

Ben's eyes widen. He gives a whistle of admiration.

"James Berkeley? You must be some actress. Isn't your agent worried about you working with him?"

"I don't have an agent," I say. "And why should I be worried?" My curiosity makes me momentarily forget that I haven't a hope in hell of ever working with James Berkeley.

"Haven't you heard?" Ben waves his whisky tumbler in explanation. "Berkeley is a crazy control freak. He dictates everything his actors and actresses do. And I mean *everything*." He emphasises the last word meaningfully. "His last film, he had a contract made up. It stated that he choose who his leading lady dated."

"What?" Lorna is horrified. She's always had a crush on Berkeley.

Ben nods. "I heard it through a friend of hers. He made her sign, insisting she only date men he had pre-approved, or he wouldn't work with her."

The shock of all this is weaving through me.

"He sounds insane," I say finally, trying to remember the serious man I met earlier.

Ben nods. "Insane, and insanely talented. All his leads get Oscars. I guess if you're an actress, you have to make the call. Is an Oscar worth a few months of hell?"

I nod slowly, acknowledging the truth of this. Most of the students I went to drama school with would accept a lot worse than dating restrictions to be guaranteed an Oscar.

We're interrupted by a waiter, who moves discreetly beside me.

"Excuse me, madam. Are you Isabella Green?"

"Yes." I feel my stomach lurch, wondering what I've done wrong.

"The gentleman over there has asked that I serve you and your friends a glass of Dom Perignon and requested that you might join him by yourself."

"Gentleman? Which gentleman?" I ask, staring over to where he's pointing. There's nothing in that direction but the low-lights of the Super VIP booths.

"The gentleman in the booth nearest the window." He points to the largest booth. "Mr James Berkeley."

Chapter 6

"Oh my God!" Lorna's voice nearly takes the roof of the club off. She's eyeing me suspiciously. "I *knew* he must have liked you, the way you were acting."

"Shhh," I mutter, alive with embarrassment as people look over at us.

"Go! Go!" shouts Lorna, pushing me towards the VIP area. "Before the waiter forgets you were the one he asked."

I stumble forward, feeling like Cinderella in her glass slippers as I totter after the waiter in my fake-designer shoes.

I try not to stare into the booths as I pass the stern-looking bodyguards, but I'm sure I catch a glimpse of at least three Hollywood actors and several famous models as I walk past.

The final booth is the largest, and it's also the emptiest.

Sat inside is Berkeley, alone, but somehow managing to fill the entire area. He is dark, brooding and looks serious. For a moment, the nerves threaten to overwhelm me. *This must be what it feels like to be summoned to the headmaster's office*, I think.

"Miss Green." His voice is both a greeting and a reprimand. "Take a seat."

I slide into the booth, my heart pounding. What could he possibly want?

He sits a few feet away, but just like in the theatre, he feels so much closer.

Just the thought of our proximity is enough to start the heat rising in my cheeks.

"That's a lovely dress," he says. "Guishem, if I'm not mistaken."

There's that accent again. That English aristocracy accent which is so sure about everything.

"It's borrowed," I admit, wondering how he can radar in on my inadequacies with such accuracy. He makes a quiet glance at my shoes but says nothing.

I assume since he can name the designer who made my dress, he knows instantly that my footwear is fake.

"I noticed you were talking with Ben Gracey," he says.

"Yes."

He is silent for a moment.

"You should be careful around him," he says.

I raise my eyebrows in disbelief, remembering Ben's comment that Berkeley is a control freak.

"What exactly do you mean?" I say stiffly.

"Exactly that." His voice is clipped.

"Are you trying to tell me who I should associate with?"

My voice has raised an octave in affront. Ok, so I was a little wary of Ben Gracey myself. But it's certainly none of Berkeley's business.

"No," he says. His eyes look tired suddenly. "I wouldn't dream of telling you what to do, Isabella."

"Then why have you called me over here?" I demand.

His expression changes back to amusement.

"I enjoyed your audition today, Isabella, but I'm still baffled by you. I thought we might have a conversation which would help me learn more about you as an actress."

Nothing to know, I think, recalling my lack of experience.

"You grew up in England?" he asks, cocking his head slightly.

"Yes."

"As did I," he looks thoughtful. "For a time, at least."

In the pause that follows, I notice that he's ditched the director's blacks in favour of jeans, a vintage T-shirt, and a suit jacket which fits his broad shoulders and muscular chest to the millimetre.

I find myself imagining what it would be like to run my hands inside the jacket.

"Do you like wine?" he says. His voice is less stern.

"I… I don't drink," I manage to stutter. To my relief, he accepts this without question.

"A soft drink? Water?"

"Yes. Yes please. Water."

He gestures to the waiter and issues instructions with the graceful simplicity of someone used to being served.

In the booth next to us is a sudden explosion of noise. The group has ordered a treasure chest – a hewn out trunk into which is poured bottle after bottle of Champagne and spirits, and set off with sparklers.

I've never seen this particular drink order up close, but Lorna has described in detail how they cost £1000 each and are the flashiest item at the bar.

Berkeley frowns slightly.

"A waste of good Champagne," he mutters.

Another cork pops and the table of people whoop and cheer.

Our drinks arrive. His is a whisky tumbler with a few perfectly square cubes of clinking ice in a dash of golden liquid. He waits for me to pick mine up before raising his to his lips. *His lips.* I am staring again.

"I wanted to dig a little deeper into your character, Isabella," he says, back in stern mode again.

"Yes?" I take a little sip of iced water.

"I was interested to see you act." That word again. Interested. Hardly the greatest compliment of my acting career.

"You mentioned you had never tried for a lead role," he continues, taking a sip of whisky. He pauses for a second, savouring the drink. "Is it your ambition to have a career in theatre?"

I nod. My mouth is dry.

He looks slightly disappointed.

"A stage actress then," he decides.

"No," I shake my head. "Well, not really," I clarify. "I majored in script writing. I always wanted to write for the stage. It was only towards my final year I got pulled into more performances."

"So you don't want to act?" he looks genuinely baffled.

"I like to act," I say slowly. "But I'm not sure it's where my talent lies." I give him an apologetic smile. "All the students I did drama with at college -they all love getting up in front of people. Being the centre of attention. I'm not like that. So I don't think I'm the right personality," I conclude, "to make it as a career actress. But I would like to play some parts, to understand more about writing."

I'm thinking back to the earlier audition, knowing I'm right. The rejection was so painful. I couldn't live like actors do. I'm not strong enough.

"I see." Berkeley takes another sip of whisky. He looks much older for a moment, though I know he can't be very old. The young director award he won could only have been awarded to a man under forty.

He turns to face me and I find myself caught in his green eyes.

"Have you ever considered acting in a movie?" he says.

I shake my head, mesmerised by what he might say next.

"I would like you to consider it," he says. "I may have a part in mind for you," he continues.

What?

The suggestion takes me completely by surprise. I sit, stunned, trying to let what he's just said sink in. James Berkeley is suggesting I act in one of his movies?

For a brief moment, I feel as though all my Christmases have come at once. And ashamed as I am to admit it, most of my joy comes from the idea of spending more time with him. With James Berkeley.

Then reality floods in, and I frown. This can't be as good as it sounds. Besides, I never had any ambition to act in movies. What if I'm terrible on-screen? The thought is too awful to contemplate, and I feel my courage slipping away.

"Do you mean a part in one of your movies?" I whisper. I am still reeling with shock. Never in a million years did I imagine this happening.

He nods curtly, and I feel another surge of amazed joy rise up.

I push it down. There must be some catch. Why should he want to cast me? I've never acted in a movie before. I could let him down.

"But first you must understand I am not an easy man to work for."

Right. There's the catch.

I remember Ben's comments, about him controlling who his actresses dated. *No way*, some defiant part in me hisses, *I don't want to work for someone like that.*

"I am looking for a new talent," he continues, "something fresh… and innocent. I think that could be you." His voice is soft.

Wow. Fresh and innocent. That's personal. How does he know I'm fresh and innocent?

"What do you mean by difficult to work with?" I manage.

He stares at me. "Difficult," he says. "But I hope rewarding. If you decide to accept my offer, I will tell you more about my conditions."

"I don't understand," I say, "are you offering me a part?"

"So long as you can agree to my terms," he says. "And I need you to trust it is the right part for you."

What?

"I won't tell you any more about it until you decide to accept," he continues.

What the hell does he have in mind?

My type-casting comes back to me. Is he going to cast me in some erotic role and make me sign away my rights before I know what I'm doing?

I dismiss the thought as ridiculous, but my distrust must show in my face.

"What are your concerns?" he asks.

"Is there any nudity?" I say and, as the words come out of my mouth, I flush a deep red at how stupid I sound.

He looks surprised.

"Have you seen my movies, Isabella?"

Of course I've seen your movies.

"Yes."

"Then why would you think nudity was involved? It's not been a habit of mine to shoot nude sex scenes."

His voice sounds bemused, but the expression on his face is unreadable.

I stare down at the soft leather of the booth, mortified.

"It's just that I often get asked to do those kind of seductress roles," I mutter.

"You do?" I look up to see his eyebrows raised. His features have shifted. He looks angry. "Who by?" His crisp English tones make the question sound dangerous.

"At college," I sigh, trying to explain. "It's because I'm half-Spanish. I always get picked to do the femme fatales and the villainesses."

Both of these are so far away from my real persona it's laughable. I've barely even gone all the way with a guy and people think I'm a seductress. But that's what dark hair and grey eyes get you.

"I see," he says. "But a femme fatale is different from being asked to act nude. Has someone ever requested you act nude?" His voice is tight.

I shake my head vehemently, shocked by the question.

"Good," he says, and the anger in his voice has abated. "In your case it would be completely unnecessary," he adds.

I look up at him, wondering what he means.

"I will wait until tomorrow for you to think about us working together," he says. "I don't wish you to rush the decision, but I am not a patient man and I have a schedule."

Work together.

The idea brings a flash of pleasure. I shake it away. This man is a control freak who dictates his actresses' personal lives. And it's not like I crave an Oscar.

"There is one more thing," he says, and the tone of his voice is almost apologetic.

I put down my glass of water, intrigued by the sudden softening. "What?" I ask.

"If we are working together," he says, "nothing can happen between us."

I stare back at him in total shock. It would never have occurred to me that such a thought would have crossed his mind.

"Of course not," I mumble, "you're married."

He blinks in surprise, and then breaks into a surprisingly warm smile.

"I'm not married, Isabella," he says.

I frown in confusion, and he continues.

"It's a Hollywood marriage," he says. "A marriage of convenience. Mainly for Madison's convenience," he adds, "to help her career."

My head is spinning.

He married someone, to further their career. What does that say about his morals?

"We never took any vows," he adds, "there was never any ceremony. I believe in marriage."

I realise the disapproval must be evident on my face.

"We announced it to the press," he continues, "but Madison and I are not bound in any legal sense. I would never make a promise, which I couldn't keep."

Madison Ellis. Troubled singer, actress, nearing her forties. I guess a marriage to a famous director would help her career.

I suppose this makes quite a lot of sense, and I'm embarrassed at my naivety.

Berkeley raises his whisky glass and takes another sip.

"She was a good friend having a hard time, so we got together for the press," he says. "But there was never anything romantic between us."

I feel a whirl of emotions sweep through me. He's just let me in on what should be a very intimate secret. How does he know I won't blab it to anyone?

"It's well known on the celebrity circuit," he adds, and I feel a little stab of deflation.

"I'll think about what you said," I say, putting down my glass. Suddenly, everything feels too much. Him telling me he's not interested in me then revealing he's available after all has come like a juggernaut. I want to crawl away and turn it all around in my mind. Although I hate to admit it, the rejection hurts.

This is the only man I've ever had such strong feelings for. And he's a celebrity crush who could have any woman in the world. What does that say about me? What's wrong with me?

"Isabella," he says quietly. I look into his green eyes. "I didn't tell you there could be nothing between us to hurt you."

"Why did you then?" I whisper, mentally planning my exit from the booth.

"Do you remember when you were acting Juliet?" he says softly. His gaze is steady, intense. I swallow and nod.

"You broke off the scene after a few lines," I say, unable to keep the accusation from my voice. "You didn't think I was good enough."

He shakes his head slowly. His expression is suddenly charged.

"I thought you were good enough," he says, leaning back very slightly in his chair. I have the sudden sensation of being prey in the presence of a predator.

His eyes look wicked, hungry.

"I broke off the scene early because I am a professional," he says. "I do not become involved with my actresses."

The way he says *my* actresses sounds possessive. It sends a warning bolt through me.

"And I knew if we had carried out the rest of that scene, acting together," he continues, leaning forward in the booth, "I would have taken you, right there, on the stage."

Waves of hot shock roll through my body.

Does he mean what I think he means?

To my embarrassment, my body betrays me. The words have an instant effect and I feel myself growing warm everywhere. I wonder if he knows. I blush furiously at the thought. But my mind is a sudden riot of images of just how James Berkeley might have had me on the stage.

"Think about my offer," he says, the stern tone returning to his voice. "I will be in contact tomorrow."

I move uncertainly to my feet, his words still sending shockwaves through my brain. It feels as though I have pins and needles in my legs, and I lean for a moment on the table.

"Are you alright?" he asks, concern spiking in his voice.

"I'm fine," I say, righting myself. "I'm not used to such high heels."

"Just be careful around Ben Gracey," he says. His eyes are full of feeling suddenly. "I know more about him than you do."

"Who I spend my time with is none of your business," I say.

Yet, gloats some evil voice in my mind. I dismiss it. I don't think I want to work for James Berkeley and that's that.

Turning from him, I stalk with as much dignity as I can manage back to where Lorna has now amassed a bevy of male admirers.

But behind me I feel a pair of green eyes boring into my back.

The evening passes in a whirl as Lorna and Ben flirt, and I brood over James Berkeley's words. *A part in a movie.*

Then before I know it, the lights have gone down, and we're in the scrum of people trying to get a black cab home.

"Come on," says Ben, tugging Lorna with him. "Let's get a mini cab." Lorna has had a few glasses of Champagne too many, and totters uncertainly behind him.

"Wait," I say. "Isn't it dangerous to take an unlicensed car?"

Ben gives a lopsided smile, born of plenty of whisky.

"We'll be fine," he says, throwing out his arm to signal a car.

A battered-looking Ford slows, and the driver winds down his window, giving us a smile filled with gold-teeth.

"I'm not sure about this," I hiss to Ben. "We were always told to take a black cab. An unlicensed cab is like getting into a stranger's car."

I realise I'm quoting from the warning posters pasted all over London. I sound ridiculous. But I'm also anxious. This car doesn't look like the kind of vehicle which we should be riding home in.

"Relax, Isabella," says Ben, and I realise from his eyes that he really has had a lot to drink. "You're with me."

"Wait!" I say, but he's already moving to the cab.

"Come on, Issy," says Lorna, her eyes pleading with me not to make a fuss. She obviously likes Ben.

"Ok," I say, taking an uncertain step towards the car.

Ben mutters a few words to the driver, then opens the door and slides into the front seat. Lorna opens the back door. Suddenly, it is slammed shut by another hand.

I turn around in shock.

James Berkeley is standing by the car. His palm is flat on the battered door where he's shut it, and I have never seen a man look so angry.

His fury is so intense that I take a step back. Even Lorna, who is un-phased by anything, and tipsy in any case, gives him a timid smile.

"Hey," she says, "you look familiar."

"What do you think you're doing?" says James. His voice is tight with fury. At first, I think he is angry with me. And then I see his words are directed at Ben.

In the passenger seat, Ben's drunken grin subsides a little.

"Berkeley," he says, "long time, no see."

Long time no see. So they know each other. I log the fact against the earlier conversations.

"Do not tell me you were about to take these girls in this unlicensed death trap?" James is glowering. Ben's smile fades completely.

"I… It's not a big deal," he says. "We can't all have our own drivers," he adds, with something like bitterness in his voice.

"These girls are not getting in that car," says James. And without waiting for a response, he steers Lorna and me to his own BMW, which I now see is pulled up behind us on the street.

Before I have time to think it through, he's delivered Lorna into the backseat and steers me by the waist behind her. Inside, I see that Lorna is entering the sleepy phase of drunk. I sigh. Ok. Better to get in and get her home.

Berkeley closes the door softly on the leather interior and takes a seat in the front, even though there's plenty of room in the back.

There's a thick screen of blackened glass between us, but after a moment this slides down, and James and his driver are revealed on the other side.

"I… Um. We live in Chelsea," I manage, wondering about Ben left alone in the other cab.

"I know where you live," growls James.

He does?

"Promise me you won't ever consider getting in an unlicensed car again. No matter what the incentive," he adds, with a meaningful glance at Lorna, who is now dozing gently on my shoulder. "Terrible things happen to girls who look like you," he adds.

I nod, not knowing what else to do. And seeming satisfied with this, Berkeley eases up the glass window, leaving us alone in the back.

When we pull up outside our apartment, he helps us both out of the car.

"Will she be alright?" he asks, looking at Lorna, who has sobered up but is blinking with the sleepiness of having just woken up.

"Yes," I say, "she'll be fine. I'll get her straight to bed. She's just tired."

"And what about you?" his green eyes are resting on mine. "Doesn't seem like much of a fun night out for you, babysitting your friend whilst she picks up unsuitable men."

I shrug. What can I say? I'm used to it.

He seems to read my answer from my expression.

"Alright then," he says. "If you're sure you don't need help getting in, I won't intrude on your time further."

And with that, he's back in his car, and it pulls away.

"Hey," says Lorna, more awake now. "Didn't he look like James Berkeley?"

Chapter 7

"Lorna, wake up." I am standing by her bed holding a plate of toasted bagel and sliced fruit.

She groans and rolls over, pulling the sheets over her head.

"Lorna Hamilton, wake up this instant!" I put on my best head-teacher voice. "You need to check your blood sugar levels."

Lorna pulls the sheet down and claps her hand to her head. Despite crashing at 3am last night in full make-up, she looks surprisingly fresh-faced.

"Here." I hand her the bagel, and the little puncture device she uses to check her blood. Lorna takes it, looks at it accusingly, and then jabs a pin-prick of blood from her finger onto a card.

I look away. I can't stand the sight of blood.

"Done?" I ask, my head turned from the bed.

"Yep. All fine, see?" Lorna shows me the reading.

"Even so," I say. "No more alcohol, Lorna. It could be dangerous."

"Just a couple of glasses of Champagne," protests Lorna. "It's fine."

She thinks for a moment. "How did I get home?"

"We got a lift back with a friend of mine," I say. "Ben Gracey was keen to take you home though. We were halfway into an unlicensed car with him when my friend pulled up."

"Oh," she looks at me. "Did Ben get my number?"

She's clearly too smitten with Ben to question that I had a friend who drove us home. Which suits me just fine. Right now, I'm not up for answering questions about the confusing Mr Berkeley.

"I don't know. Probably. He was into you."

There's a sudden ringing in the apartment. We both look at each other. The doorbell. A very unfamiliar sound, since most post is held by the concierge downstairs.

"I'll get it." I put the plate of bagels by Lorna's bed and head for the door.

I pull it back to see a delivery man holding a huge box and figure Ben must have tracked down Lorna's address and sent flowers. That kind of thing often happens to her.

"Package for Isabella Green?" says the delivery man.

"That's me," I say in surprise.

"Here," he says, handing me the box. It's enormous and I need both hands to hold it. I sign and take the mysterious package back into Lorna's bedroom.

"What is it?" she says, sitting up in bed.

"I don't know." I set the package down on the floor. It's large and light turquoise, with a huge white bow wrapped around.

"Open it! Open it!"

Very slowly, I tug off the big bow, eliciting a groan of frustration from Lorna.

"How can you stand to do it so slowly?" she complains. I smile and ease off the top of the huge box.

Inside are three more boxes. I stare at the familiar names. The largest one is a black Chanel box. The second is smaller and soft grey, embossed with the words 'Jimmy Choo".

Lorna claps her hands to her mouth.

"Oh my God!" she whispers. "They're from him, aren't they? James Berkeley?"

I'm shaking my head. But I can't think where else they might be from.

There's a small card and I slide it out of the heavy cream paper envelope.

"Read it!" demands Lorna.

I lower my eyes to the curved inked writing and read the words.

"I thought you might appreciate an outfit you didn't have to borrow. This will ensure you don't worry about the dress code. I've booked a table at The Ivy for 1pm. I'll send a car to your apartment. Don't be late."

I drop the card and stare at Lorna.

"It's from Berkeley. He's sent me clothes and booked a table at The Ivy for lunch today."

"The Ivy!" she says. "It takes three months to get a table there, even if you know someone."

I nod. Of course I know this. The Ivy is the favourite lunch location of celebrities all over the world. The average person doesn't stand a hope of getting a table, and even those with contacts usually have to wait. How did he get a table so quickly?

"Perhaps he booked it months ago," I say, knowing the reasonableness of this, but feeling a little depressed by it. Most likely James Berkeley planned to take a date and has filled me in last minute.

But Lorna is shaking her head.

"You have to say who is coming to make the booking," she says. "It's restaurant policy. They like to welcome each guest by name."

Oh.

"So…" says Lorna. "He must have spent this morning arranging the booking and buying you gifts." She looks at her watch. "And it's only 10:30am so he's been hard at it. Open them!" she adds, seeing me hesitate before the sumptuous packages.

I open the Chanel box. Inside are a beautiful dark grey suit and a cream Miss Moneypenny-style blouse.

I look up at Lorna. "A Chanel suit," I say as I draw out the perfectly-cut wool jacket. "Does he expect me to wear this?" The skirt is the same soft grey wool as the jacket, and the slightly transparent blouse is light silk with long ties falling from the neck. It's much more formal than anything I'd usually wear.

"Looks like it," says Lorna. She picks up a bagel and takes a bite.

I open the next box, labelled Jimmy Choo, embarrassed to think he recognised my fakes and bought me replacements.

Inside is a pair of high-heeled peephole shoes in patent black leather.

Lorna raises her eyebrows. "Sexy," she says. "Are you sure he wants to talk about work?"

I let out a puff of air in answer and move on to the third package.

Marc Jacobs. It's a bag made of butter-soft leather, fixed with an array of perfectly-placed buckles. The colour is not what I would have chosen – a subtle green – but I can see instantly it's the perfect match for the suit and my light grey eyes.

I sit for a moment staring at the array of gifts. I know without even adding up the cost that it's more than I've been given in my whole life.

"I can't accept this," I decide. "It's too much. And besides, who does that Lorna? Who dictates what someone wears to a lunch appointment?"

I remember his reputation as a control freak.

I shake my head. "I'm going to tell him to stuff his lunch appointment and his dress code."

It's then I realise I don't have his number. *Damn.*

Wait. How did he know where I live?

He must have taken the information from the theatre, I realise. Surely that's against data protection? Then again, I did leave details so I could be contacted about the audition. And this is about work. Right?

"I'll ignore the car," I decide. "Arrogant idiot. Who does he think he is, sending clothes and arranging lunch without asking me?"

"Perhaps it's another audition," says Lorna, "a test?"

My curiosity is piqued. "What kind of test?"

"Well, you know. You said he wouldn't tell you the role. What if he wants to play it out over lunch? And the clothes are so you can get into character?"

I consider this. It doesn't sound *too* crazy. But do I want all this? This strange world of gifts and rules I don't understand?

"Go," says Lorna. "What's the worst that could happen? You get a free outfit."

I bristle. "I don't want his clothes, Lorna."

"An experience then. You've missed out on so much, Issy, since, you know, the thing in that bar."

The thing in the bar. The reason I don't drink alcohol. We hardly ever talk about it, but Lorna knows how much it affects me.

"Be brave," she says, "try something different. And besides, honey, it's The Ivy! Most of us will never get to go. At least go along and tell me what the food's like."

Against my own best advice, I am readying myself for the car when it pulls up outside my flat.

A black BMW. Typical.

Damn. I check my watch. Ten minutes earlier than I expected. And I'm still cramming my change purse and phone and make-up into the unfamiliar designer bag.

It's another five minutes before I make it out to the car. The driver opens the door, and I slide in gratefully.

"You're late." The deep voice makes me start, and I turn to see James Berkeley only a few feet away.

Jeez.

"I… I thought I was meeting you at the restaurant," I say, marvelling at how thoroughly this man always manages to wrong-foot me.

He raises his eyebrows. "And leave a lady to arrive at a restaurant alone? I'm a gentleman, Isabella. Of course I would personally escort you. Who knows who might run off with you between the car and restaurant?" he adds, with a roguish grin.

I smile despite myself. He's joking.

The driver slides the car into gear and pulls out onto the Chelsea streets.

"Nice location for an apartment," he says, looking admiringly at the classic façade of my building.

"My father left it to me," I say. "But the service charge is the same as rent." I give a rueful shrug. "So, it's not helped my graduate cash-flow."

He looks thoughtful. "Surely someone can negotiate you out of that contract?" he says.

"They could, but my mother has the legal papers," I say. "Legality isn't her thing."

"Do you work?" he asks.

What a question. Of course I work. But Berkeley was sent to boarding school in England, so he's probably used to people with trust funds.

"Yes," I reply, "I work as a waitress for Kinglys. We cater to silver service events."

The car pulls through Chelsea, past the boutique clothing stores and restaurants, and swings onto the road which passes Buckingham Palace.

"Look," I say, feeling suddenly braver in his company. "What did you mean by the suit?"

"The suit?" he makes a comedy assessment of his own perfect suit jacket.

"This suit," I say, pulling meaningfully at my tailored wool lapel. "And the shoes, and the bag?"

"You don't like them?"

"No... I. It's not that. They're lovely," I admit. "And I have no idea how you got the perfect fit."

His mouth twitches. "I am observant," he says, "of beautiful things."

Does he mean the suit?

"But what do you mean by them?" I press. "Is this some weird audition thing?"

"Some weird audition thing?" he looks genuinely hurt. "Of course not. I'm not interested in dressing you. I simply assumed you would be more comfortable, since our appointment was such short notice, if I took out the effort of the dress code. And I couldn't be sure the friend who had so generously lent you that beautiful dress would be so accommodating this morning."

"Oh." This sounds very gentlemanly, but I am still suspicious.

"And do you always supply your lunch appointments with outfits?"

"I have never made a lunch appointment at this short notice," he says. "A table of recently-signed musicians have been very disappointed today."

I gape at him. "But that's... It's not fair," I protest. "We can't take someone else's table."

He smiles. "Just a little joke, Isabella. The Ivy always keeps back a table for me should I require it."

"Oh." I am a little thrown. Berkeley doesn't seem like the kind of man who makes jokes. "Why is that?"

"I was one of the founders of the restaurant," he says, leaning forward in the car. "You really do look very beautiful in that suit," he adds, lowering his voice. "Very sophisticated. Perfect for lunch. Perhaps one day I will be fortunate enough to see you dressed for dinner."

Whoa. Is he asking me out to dinner? This is confusing.

One minute, he's saying nothing can happen between us. Now, he seems to be flirting. Does he mean it? Or is he joking again?

"I can't keep the clothes and the bag," I say, determined to bring the conversation back to within the realms of my control. "It was lovely of you to think of them, but I wouldn't feel right."

Berkeley shrugs. "All those designers have a strict policy on seconds," he says. "If they are returned then they will be destroyed. It would seem a shame to cause the destruction of such well-made objects."

He lets the sentence hang in the air, but I refuse to be drawn.

"You should have thought about that before you bought them," I say.

His face shifts as though he's trying to supress a smile.

"Keep them for today," he says. "See how you feel tomorrow."

The car winds silently towards the curb, and I realise we've reached our destination.

The Ivy's white and black entrance looms. I've seen it before, walking around London, but I never imagined I would get to go inside.

"Wait here," says Berkeley. For a moment, I think he's getting out to pay the driver. But of course, this is his own member of staff.

Then I realise he has darted round to the far side of the car to open the door for me.

Is this a date?

The thought slides into my head as he offers his hand to help me out. I twist my legs out of the car, keeping my knees together, and use his strong arm to right myself.

For a split second, we stand facing each other, and then he positions my arm carefully alongside his to guide us both inside.

The warmth of his body close to mine makes butterflies in my stomach.

"After you, Miss Green," he says, pushing the door, and giving me my first sight of The Ivy's fabulous art nouveau interior.

There is glass everywhere, and the walls are decked in paintings and screen-prints I recognise to be by Damien Hirst and Lucien Freud.

I stand lost for a moment as the maître de approaches. And then he recognises Berkeley and the two shake hands.

We are shown to a table at the back of the restaurant, a distance from the other diners.

"Please," Berkeley pulls my chair, and I sit.

"Thanks," I say as he seats himself opposite.

"You look quite at home here," he says with a slight smile. "Have you been before?"

Quite at home? I'm so out of place even the waiters must notice.

"Of course not," I mutter, looking up at him. "Mr Berkeley, are you mocking me?"

He looks surprised. "Isabella, I am not. You appear at exclusive launch parties in designer dresses. And you reside in a Chelsea flat. I assume you are *au fait* with London's better dining establishments."

He hasn't asked me to call him by his first name, I notice. Not a date then. The thought disappoints me, although he's already explained he's not interested in me.

And then he said he wanted to have you on the stage, whispers a dangerous voice in my head. I shake it away.

"The dress was borrowed," I say, "and the apartment was inherited with an enormous service charge and nothing else."

A waiter appears at Berkley's side and presents him with a wine list. His eyes flick down to it and then back up at me.

"Would you like wine with your lunch? They have an excellent Chablis which is an ideal accompaniment to the scallops."

"No thank you," I say.

He pauses for a second as if to disagree, and then he hands the menu back the waiter.

"Something to discuss later, perhaps," he says, almost to himself.

The waiter makes to hand him the food menu, but he waves it politely away.

"I already know the menu," he says. "We'll have the scallops to start with and then the lamb to follow." He thinks for a moment. "And a glass of the Haut Medoc Grand Cru with the lamb," he adds, pronouncing the French words with fluent flair.

The waiter vanishes, and I scowl at him.

"You do know what year it is?" I say. "Women order their own food nowadays."

He smiles. "But you've never been here, Isabella. And I know what is best to eat. So, in this instance, you'll defer to my judgement."

He sits back and folds his hand.

"Have you thought about my proposition?"

The way he says it, it sounds like a marriage proposal.

"Between 11pm last night and when a package of clothes arrived this morning? I've not had a great deal of time," I say.

He smiles. "A very reasonable answer."

"And," I take a breath, "I don't think I can agree."

His face falls. "Oh?"

"I'm very new to all this, Mr Berkeley." I spread my hands out on the table. "I don't have any idea what's normal and what's not. But I don't think this is a usual way to cast actresses."

"You're very perceptive."

"I'd be a fool not to be interested," I continue. "I've seen your films and I know the kind of critical acclaim they generate." I sigh. "You must be an interesting person to work with, and I would like to see how you make a movie."

"But?" He leans forward.

"But. I can't agree to your terms. I can't take a role on trust, not knowing what it is. I'm not experienced enough to take that risk. I might let you down. And I hardly know anything about you," I add.

And what I do know isn't good.

I sit back, having said my piece, and almost as soon as I do, two waiters arrive and place a plate of scallops in front of each of us.

They smell delicious, and I hesitate for a moment before Berkeley nods I should pick up my fork. I spear a mouthful and take a nervous bite of the first scallop, conscious he is watching me. It is predictably delicious, with a firm flesh texture and a ginger-butter sauce.

"You like them?"

"They're delicious."

Berkeley nods approvingly, then picks up his fork and spears the white flesh of the first morsel. He waits a moment, the fork poised, and then speaks.

"You say you don't know anything about me. What would you like to know?" he says evenly.

This throws me completely.

"How do you know Ben Gracey?" I say, speaking the first thing which comes into my head. His expression darkens a little.

"He's a relative," he says. "On my father's side. A cousin."

That makes sense. The English aristocracy are all interrelated. Judging from his accent, Berkeley is probably a distant relative of every noble-born person in England.

"Where are you from? Why do you work in Hollywood?" I ask, opting for my most pressing questions.

"I was born in Mauritius," he says, taking a sip of wine, "and I went to boarding school in England from the age of four until I was fourteen."

"And then?"

"Then I was removed to a boarding school in Hong Kong where I became interested in theatre and movies. I made prudent movie investments in several different countries and then I moved to LA to direct and produce."

"What do you mean by removed?" I ask, surprised at my own daring.

Berkeley smiles but it doesn't reach his eyes. "Expelled," he says shortly. "Isabella, I don't talk about my past a great deal. For you, I have made this small exception. Don't push me."

The words come out pure cut-glass English aristocracy. He strikes his fork at the plate in a manner which suggests the conversation is over. I twist my mouth, upset that I've offended him.

"I'm sorry for asking, Mr Berkeley," I say. I sound like a schoolgirl.

He looks at me in surprise, assessing for a moment. He's deciding whether or not I'm teasing him.

"I like that you call me Mr Berkeley," he says, grinning as he puts a scallop into his mouth.

For some reason, the comment makes me furious. I pick up my fork and another scallop.

"So James," I say pointedly, "I know a little more about you, but I still can't agree to commit to a role I know nothing about."

I spear another scallop and ease it into my mouth.

Berkeley cocks his head a little to one side.

"Well then, Miss Green," he says. "Let's see if we might not come to some arrangement. How about I tell you the role I have in mind for you, and you agree to my other conditions on trust?"

This is unexpected.

"What's your working style?" I hedge, hoping to draw more out about what's expected of his actors and actresses.

"My working style?" He picks up a spotless napkin and dabs his mouth. "My working style, Miss Green, is all about discipline." He fixes me with a steely gaze.

I swallow my last bite of scallop.

"Discipline?"

He nods. "Discipline, Isabella, is vital to drawing the best performance from a production. I need to know that my performers are willing to give up everything, every little last decision if it comes to it, over their personal lives. This is how I extract Oscar performances from every lead I have ever worked with, and a great deal of supporting roles.

Arrogant, I think, *to credit himself with an actor's Oscar.* Although I can't help but think there is some truth to his self-grandeur. He is known as the best director, after all.

"I don't care about an Oscar," I say.

"Then what do you care about?"

I think about this. "I care about the art of it all. I care about the script and the words and how it all goes together."

His haughty expression softens.

"And you want to act to understand this all better?"

"Yes." I am surprised at how well he summarises me.

"Then there is no better place for you," he says, his voice dipping low, "than with me."

I feel my eyes open wide. Is he saying what I think he's saying? His face looks suddenly charged with lust, and I feel my body responding.

A waiter leans in and removes the scallop plates and another waiter replaces them with empty plates and a rack of lamb in the middle of the table.

The smell of the food is amazing. I hope the waiter can't see my flame-red face.

James stands and takes the carving knife, nodding that the waiter can depart.

"Rare or well done?" he asks, severing a piece of lamb with expert strokes.

"Medium, please," I mutter. He steers two pieces onto my plate and then serves himself. Then he takes a deep sip of red wine.

"Would I have to sign a contract?" I say, as much to break the unbearable silence of him watching me as anything else.

He raises his eyebrows. "Of course. All movies come with contracts."

"I don't mean that," I say. "I mean a contract for the things you mentioned. The giving up of personal control."

James takes a slice of lamb, chews and swallows.

"No, of course not," he says, sounding bemused. "It is a personal matter between myself and my performers. I have never had anyone break their word," he adds. "We would make an agreement on trust."

This is new information. So Ben Gracey had it wrong. Or Berkeley is lying.

I look at his face, trying to detect signs of dishonestly, and finding none.

"I'll think about it," I say.

He nods, but looks displeased. I feel deflated.

"How about a screen test?" he says suddenly.

I look up from my plate.

"What do you mean?"

"You agree to come to my studio tomorrow," he says. "Take a screen test, find out my working style for yourself. See how you look on screen. If you don't like the experience, then we'll part ways, no hard feelings. If you do, then we might agree to work together."

I stare at him warily. That doesn't sound too bad. Good, in fact. And in my own way, I feel as though I've scored a minor victory over Mr-Control-Freak-Berkeley. He's agreed to audition me on my own terms. Ha.

"Alright," I say, swallowing the last piece of lamb on my plate and setting my knife and fork back. "That sounds do-able."

"Do-able?"

"Do-able," I repeat. "It's a word." I pretend to narrow my eyes at him. His face breaks into a delighted smile. He looks his true age, suddenly a young man of thirty rather than forty.

Then his phone beeps and he removes it from his suit jacket and frowns.

"Nancy," he says, and I remember the name of the casting director from the theatre. The one who had to step aside for personal reasons.

He is shaking his head.

"I'm sorry," he says, signalling for the cheque, "I have to deal with this."

I lower my eyes. Of course he has more important engagements than me. I pick up the new Marc Jacobs bag feeling strangely at limbo. Part of me wants to stay in this glamorous world with this intriguing man. But I have to return to reality.

Until tomorrow, I remind myself gleefully. Tomorrow is the screen test. The nerves in the pit of my stomach blend with delicious excitement at the thought.

We step outside the restaurant and his car pulls up. "My car will take you anywhere you need to go," he says, hailing a taxi.

The black cab slows, and James turns to face me. "Until tomorrow?" he says, and his voice sounds urgent.

I nod, confused yet again by his intentions.

He takes my shoulders and leans in to cheek-kiss me, brushing his lips with deliberate slowness against my right cheekbone, and then my left.

"Until tomorrow," he murmurs, his breath stroking through my hair. He waits there for a second, holding me pinned inside his arms, and then he steps back and stares into my eyes.

For a moment, I think he's about to say something else. And then he gives a quick little nod, and he's gone.

I feel every muscle of my body sigh out after him as he slides into the cab.

I get into his car and ask the driver to take me back to Chelsea.

As I sink back into the leather seats, I realise I can smell him on the interior.

James Berkeley, I think, inhaling his fragrance deep into my lungs, *what have you done to me?*

Chapter 8

Late as ever, I wrestle into my Kingley's uniform. The black and white waitress outfit was bought out of my own wages and is the cheapest I could get away with.

My friend Jerome has already clocked in for me and is waiting outside with the other milling staff when I emerge from the dressing room.

Jerome is my kind-of-ex-boyfriend. He took a course in theatre production in the same college as me, and we became good friends in the first year. He's blonde, good-looking, always smells great and gives the world's best hugs.

He's usually employed to put up lighting rigs in London theatres, but he also waiters with me on the side. A choice I often fear is due to him wanting us to get together again rather than a real need for spare cash.

"Hey, Issy," he says, "there's been a change of plan for tonight. We're being taken by coach to another part of the city."

I stare back at him in confusion. "A change of plan?"

"Maybe someone messed up," he says. "In any case, our shift is being driven over to Claridges to fill in for some private party there. Perhaps some other agency let them down," he adds. "In any case, we get a shift at London's fanciest hotel. Probably they'll feed us well at the end of it."

We clamber into the coach and Jerome, as usual, sits a little too close. My fault, really. A long time ago at college, I decided I had waited long enough for Mr Right. So on my mother's advice, I tried dating a good friend – Jerome. We had fun going out, and kissing him wasn't bad. Nice, really. But no strong feelings came with it.

After a few drinks at a party, I even got brave enough to try and lose my virginity to him. And then I freaked and confessed that I only saw him as a friend.

Poor Jerome has been hoping ever since that I'll give him another chance.

"You been to Claridges before, Issy?"

I think for a moment. "Yeah. I think one of my first shifts was at Claridges. They don't let you too near the guests. They have their own trained staff for that."

"Just put the food down and get out of there?"

"Yep."

"Great. If we're lucky and their in-house team has shined all the silverware, we might get out early."

We filter off the coach into the car park that Claridges reserve for their staff. Guests come in the front and the ambassadors and royalty have a red carpet rolled out. Round the back it's plain, functional and decidedly unglamorous.

We move into the kitchen and the general manager comes down to brief us. It's a straight-forward private party, serving canapés, topping up drinks. There's no food for us at the end, but as Jerome predicted, we might get out early if the guests don't stay late.

I load up with my first tray of canapés – quails eggs topped with an artful smear of caviar – and follow the rest of the team into the room. Jerome is ahead, carrying two trays. He's always been a show-off.

Claridges' wide ballroom swings into view, and as always, I'm struck by the contrast between the incredible gold and blue décor with the plain staff quarters below stairs.

My eyes sweep the room, searching for a route where other waiters have not yet been. And then I nearly drop my tray.

James Berkeley is standing, talking with another female guest.

My legs almost propel me straight back out of the room. But I'm at work. I'm holding a tray of food. Somehow, I have to get through this without him seeing me. It's not just the embarrassment of serving him. Waitress-chic I am not. My thoughts flick to my hair, scraped back into a functional bun, and my face, completely devoid of make-up. I look terrible.

Why should I care if I look terrible?

But I know the truth. I'm falling for him. And it's important he doesn't see me looking plain and awful. I'll analyse that later. Right now, I need to keep out of his way. Keeping my eyes front, I head for the opposite side of the room.

My tray lightens as I whirl through the guests, waiting for them to take food from the tray. And I turn to head back to the kitchen.

Maybe I can get away with this after all. He might not stay long.

"Isabella."

I turn. It's him, looking immaculate in a grey suit and tie.

"Oh," I swallow. "Hello Mr Berkeley."

He smiles. "Back to Mr Berkeley?"

"James," I correct myself. The weight of the tray in my hand suddenly feels unbearable, and I realise the heat of serving the room has left a sheen of sweat on my face.

He lowers his voice. "I like the way you look in your waitress's uniform."

Oh.

"I obviously chose the right catering company."

The penny drops.

"You?" I say. "You booked my catering company for this event?"

"I assumed, since you work for them, they must be the best."

I look down at the tray in my hand. A real part of me wants to hit him over the head with it.

My voice comes out as a hiss. "You hired my catering company so I would come and wait on you? What kind of twisted thing is that to pull?"

His face shows hurt, but I'm far beyond sympathy.

I look left and right to check no one can see us.

"I cannot believe you would do this!"

James takes my arm. Much to my own annoyance, the hold sends a thrill coursing through me.

"So you have a temper," he says. "That's good to see in an actress. But this isn't what you think."

Isn't it? Confusion sets in. Surely this is another one of his bizarre controlling mind games? Like sending clothes for a lunch date.

"Then what is it?" I manage, the anger in my voice lessening slightly. His hand on my arm is confusing.

"Come with me." Still gripping my upper arm, he begins leading me from the room.

"I'm working," I protest.

James makes a quick sweep of the room, signals with his hand, and in an instant the general manager is with us.

"Is there a problem, Mr Berkeley?" he asks, looking to me and to James.

"Not at all," says James. "But I am looking to cast a waitress as an extra in a film, and I think this young lady would be perfect. Would you mind if I took her away for a few moments to discuss the role?"

The manager's eyes bulge slightly. "Of course," he says. "She has my permission to be away from the shift for as long as you need her."

James nods a 'thank you' and drops his hand to propel me forward by the small of my back out of the ballroom. As we reach the entrance, he seamlessly takes the tray from my hand and hands it to a waiter travelling in the opposite direction.

"My suite is just along here," he says, pointing down the corridor and manoeuvring me forward.

"What makes you think I'm going to go in your suite with you?" I say, wondering where this is going.

He stops and turns so we are facing each other in the corridor.

"Isabella," he says, "I'm sorry if I offended you by bringing you here. Although, you really do look lovely in that uniform."

I scowl, and the corners of his mouth lift devilishly for a moment. Then his face turns serious.

"I wanted to see you," he says. "I can't stop thinking about you."

Whoa! What?

"Follow me." He propels me down the corridor again.

We arrive at an enormous door, and James slips a keycard into the holder. The suite opens up and I'm greeted with the lavish view of Claridges' priceless antique furniture and enormous four-poster bed.

"I don't have the strength," he says as we walk in the room, "to stay away from you anymore."

I'm still taking in the unexpected words when James shuts the door behind us and sweeps me suddenly into his arms, forcing me back against the door.

Then his lips are on mine and the hardness of his body is on me.

I feel an electric current surge through me. He has me pressed against the door, with one hand pinning my shoulder. My lips respond to his, moving in mirror image as his tongue flicks over my mouth. And I am sinking, sinking into him…

I force a hand between us, pushing him away.

"Wait," I say. "I can't do this."

He steps towards me again, but I keep my hand held up in warning.

"Everything with you," I gasp, "is just so confusing. You tell me nothing can happen between us, and then you book my entire catering team just to get me alone in your suite."

He nods. He is breathing heavily.

"I have never been involved with an actress, Isabella. But you…"

"Me what?"

"I have never met anyone like you," he says. "As a director, I can't let your talent go to waste. But as a man…"

He leaves the sentence hanging.

"As a man you want us to have sex?" I fill in.

"I want to do so much more to you than have sex with you," he says, and his eyes are roaming my body, hungrily.

I take a deep breath.

"James. Mr Berkeley. I have agreed to a screen test with you, and I will keep my word. But I also agreed that nothing would happen between us. If we are to work together, I don't want there to be any…" I search for the word… romantic? "Sexual involvement," I decide.

What am I saying? This is the hottest man you've ever met, and you're talking yourself out of fucking him right here, right now, in this room.

My body is virtually screaming in protest.

But that's not what I want. Not this way. And he needs to know it. I turn to leave.

"Isabella, wait."

I move to pull open the door, and he takes hold of my arm. I turn to him, my eyes challenging. Is he going to try and stop me leaving?

"If you agree to the screen test tomorrow, I agree to your terms," he says. The light has gone out of his eyes. "I think you've misjudged me," he continues, "but a gentleman does not argue with a lady."

And with a little nod of his head, he opens the door for me and lets me leave.

I half stumble down the corridor, thick with the emotion of what has just happened.

That kiss.

Half of me wants so badly to run back to the room. The other, more sensible half, walks my legs back down to the kitchen.

To my great relief, I almost crash straight into Jerome, who's sizing up which tray he can pick off canapés from to snack on.

"Hey," he says, seeing the upset in my face. "What's up? Issy? What's up?"

I fall gratefully into his arms, and he gives me one of his world-beating hugs.

"Hey," he says, "did someone out there upset you."

I nod into his shoulder. Why can't I bring myself to feel something for Jerome? He's such a lovely, uncomplicated person.

For some reason, I feel overwhelmed with emotions, and tears well up in my eyes.

What is wrong with me? A few meetings with James Berkeley and I'm a wreck. No one has ever had this effect on me.

I draw back and wipe a few tears from my cheek.

"It's nothing," I say. "Just rejecting the advances of James Berkeley."

His face does a comedic double-take.

I laugh, feeling better.

"Remember that audition Lorna got me?" I say. "It was at his theatre, and I met him then."

"Did he try to hit on you?"

"Not exactly. I think I like him. I don't know. He wants us to work together, and I don't want to complicate things. I'm fine, really."

Jerome holds my shoulders, checking in my face that I mean it.

"Well, if he bothers you, just let me know," he says, looking back out in the direction I've just come from.

I smile in thanks. Jerome is built like a quarter-back. But having just been pressed up against the wall by James, I think they'd be evenly matched.

"Thanks, it's fine, really."

"Ok." Jerome looks doubtful. "Well, let's just finish this shift, ok? Then I'll take you for a drink. Soft drink," he adds quickly, remembering.

I smile. "A soft drink sounds great."

Chapter 9

The next morning, I'm half expecting the screen test to be cancelled. Or for word never to arrive. But at 9am sharp, a hand-delivered parcel and a card in a crisp cream envelope arrives at my apartment.

A card – what's with that? If he knows my address, he must also know my mobile number.

I open it, and the same beautiful curved writing announces the screen test will be held at 4pm. A car will come to pick me up.

I unwrap the parcel. It's not tied with bows like the last package, and if I'm being truly honest with myself, I'm disappointed. Obviously, he's accepted that this is a business arrangement.

That's what you wanted, I remind myself, pulling off the brown paper.

Inside is an iPad. It's already charged, and I flick it on to see a script has been preloaded onto the screen.

Hmmm. So I guess he wants me to learn my lines.

Suddenly, my mobile rings from an unfamiliar number and I click to answer.

"Hello?"

"I take it you received my card?"

Oh. So he can use a telephone after all. His voice gives me goose bumps.

"Um. Yes."

"And you'll attend?" There's a note in his voice I haven't heard before. As though a lot rests on my reply.

I pause for a moment. "Yes," I say finally.

Is it my imagination, or do I hear a sigh of relief?

"But the conditions still apply," I continue. "I'm coming to see how you work. And to see if I can actually act this role you've got in mind. If it doesn't work, it doesn't work."

"Of course." His voice is crisp, business-like. "You are under no obligation. Come act for me and we'll take it from there."

Something about the way he says 'act for me' brings a little thrill of excitement to my body.

"Ok," I say, trying to keep my voice calm. "Then I'll see you at 4pm."

"Oh Isabella," he says gently, "I wouldn't miss it for the world."

And then the line goes dead.

I turn back to the iPad and make a quick read of the script. From my first reading, it's a love story. A young girl who charms a jaded businessman. I scan the text for bit parts and find only one female character with any lines to read. And she's a call-girl.

Great. Typecast again.

But it's a well-defined character, and I feel myself warming to the script. It's good. I wonder if this is part of his talent, picking out good scripts. Or if he has people to do that for him.

I scan through the main female character's role, searching for her connection to the smaller female part which I'm expected to play.

The process is so engrossing that time runs away with me. And before I know it, the car to take me to the audition has pulled up outside.

Quickly, I fling on a second hand floral dress, jeans, ballet pumps and a denim jacket. I cast a quick look at myself in the mirror. My dark hair falls around my shoulders, curling slightly. Not perfect, but it will have to do. I have time to apply a dab of mascara and a slick of lip gloss before running down to the waiting car.

This time, he's not inside, and my heart gives a little squeeze of sadness.

What did you expect? He's taken you at your word. No romantic involvement.

The car hums through West London before turning south towards the River Thames. We drive along part of the city known as Embankment, past the Houses of Parliament, and then east to London Bridge, where the car turns and follows the bridge over the wide River Thames.

Is the studio outside London? It would make sense.

But instead of continuing out of the city, the car turns east again, towards the fashionable dockside district of Shad Thames.

This is where London's most expensive warehouse apartments are, close to the artistic areas of Shoreditch and Brick Lane, with sweeping views across the Thames.

The car stops outside a large, converted warehouse, and the driver announces that we've arrived at our destination.

A studio based in a central London warehouse. It must cost a small fortune to run. Maybe Berkeley has smaller offices which he uses for casting.

The street outside is cobbled and lined with boutique coffee houses and tiny elegant shops. I look about in confusion. Ahead of me is an entrance of glass and steel, blending effortlessly with the warehouse.

There is a panel of buttons suggesting more than one studio within the building. Do I press one?

I'm spared the decision by the sound of someone descending a set of stairs inside.

Then the metal and glass door opens, and Berkley's handsome face is looking into mine.

His brown hair is more tousled than usual, and he's dressed casually in designer jeans and a yellow T-shirt which looks to have been bought from one of the nearby trendy boutiques. His feet are bare.

"Come in," he says, opening the door to let me through.

In the lobby of the building is a chrome elevator and equally shining set of stairs. He makes a quick assessment of both.

"We'll take the stairs," he says, and I feel my heart sink another level downwards. He doesn't even want to be alone in the elevator with me. He really has taken me at my word.

I follow him upstairs three flights and emerge in the penthouse floor. A door has been left open, and on the other side is a beautiful bare-brick apartment.

The enormous lounge is scattered with the kind of designer furniture which would cost me a year's salary a piece, and a contemporary kitchen is fitted seamlessly into the far wall.

He waves for me to go ahead and follows.

I enter, noticing as I do that an entire wall has been glassed, allowing a flowing view across the River Thames. The wedding-cake turrets of Tower Bridge are in close relief, and in the distance, London Bridge, St Pauls Cathedral and the rest of London's historic skyline are perfectly framed in the metal beams of the window.

I stop partway in, confused.

"Wait," I say, "this is your studio?"

Berkeley comes in after me, closing the door behind him.

"This is my London apartment," he says. "I have a studio room here."

I narrow my eyes at him, trying to make out whether this is professional conduct.

"I thought you were staying at Claridges," I manage, thinking of his suite.

"I stayed at Claridges last night, because I had an event I wished to host," he says. "For the most part, when I'm in London I stay here."

Oh. I allow my eyes to travel around the open room. It's stunning.

"This is a lovely apartment," I say.

"Thank you."

"Do you always conduct screen tests from your apartment?"

"This is the first time I have conducted a screen test."

He leads me over the shining floorboards of his lounge and into an equally large room at the back, where a camera and box-lights have been set-up for filming. There's a director's chair and a stage area taped to the floor, like when I first auditioned.

The memory of what he said about that first audition comes back to me, and I feel the heat in my cheeks rise.

I'm alone with James Berkeley in his apartment.

"You read the script?"

"Yes." I follow him awkwardly, uncertain of where to place myself. I have never acted to camera before.

"What was your reading of it?"

"I liked it," I say. "It was like a fairy tale. Like *Beauty and the Beast*."

He smiles and nods.

"That's exactly it," he says. "The story is a classic but told in a modern way. Fairy tales strike at the heart of human nature, Isabella. *Beauty and the Beast* tells of the redemptive power of love. Of how a broken person can be brought back to life by innocence and purity."

He's staring at me as he talks, as though there's a double-meaning to what he's saying.

"Stand there," he says, gesturing to the stage space. "And read from scene 5."

I'm clutching the iPad in my hand, and I whizz through to the scene he means. I look up at him in confusion.

"But there's only the lead female in this scene," I say. "Don't you want me to read the part I'm supposed to play?"

The side of his mouth twitches in that familiar tantalising smile. His green eyes soften slightly.

"If you remember, the lead female is the part I was thinking to cast you in," he says. "At least, if you don't object."

Did he say that? I think back to his words in the bar. *Have you ever considered a lead role?* I never assumed he meant to audition me for one.

I open my mouth to explain that I can't possibly take on a main role, and he raises a single finger to silence me.

"We agreed that you would test this out. All I ask you to do is read."

I stand with my mouth open for a moment, and then glance back down to the iPad.

Ok. You agreed to this. Might as well keep your word.

There is no doubt in my mind that this screen test will confirm to Berkeley that he was wrong about me. That I'm not lead material, and especially not in a movie. The idea of the camera close-up on my face makes me want to die.

Berkeley is behind the camera, positioning it. His gaze is down on some unseen screen, and I realise he is probably panning in on my terrified face.

I do my best to straighten my features.

The truth is, I like the lead character. She's complex and interesting. Certainly, it beats playing two-dimensional female villains.

I look back to the script. I haven't learned it this time.

"Read," commands Berkeley, and the force of his voice makes me wince.

I take a breath and plough into the lines, feeling the character as much as I am able.

Halfway through, I realise I am messing up. Berkeley is silent behind the camera, and it comes home to me that I only saw the script this morning. A professional actress might be able to commit herself to a character that quickly. But I'm just a recent graduate with hardly any experience.

I stop reading and put the iPad down. Then I look at Berkeley. He's not moving, frozen in his little world behind the camera.

"James?" I say. "Mr Berkeley?"

He looks up, and his green eyes are charged. Is he angry? The expression makes me want to back away, but at the same time it's enthralling.

He takes two steps across the small room and grabs me by the waist.

I stare up at him. Are we acting now?

"Isabella," he groans, and his voice is tight, urgent. "I think we need to renegotiate what we arranged in my suite last night."

"What?" I am held in his arms. The force of his emotion is overwhelming.

He leans closer to me so that our lips are almost touching.

"If you had any idea how beautiful you look on that screen…" he says.

Me? Beautiful?

"I refuse to let your talent go to waste," he says, wrapping his arms around the small of my back and dragging me in closer.

I am powerless, pinioned in his strong arms. I couldn't wriggle free even if I wanted to.

"But I can't work each day, watching you on that screen, and not have you at the end of it."

The words come out as a growl, and he lifts me off the ground, carrying me into another room in the apartment.

A bed comes into view just as he throws me onto it. Then he's on top of me, pinning me down.

Wait. Do I want this?

In the tumult of emotions, every sense in my body is alive. I realise I'm powerless to resist my own needs. I walked away in the suite. I haven't the strength to push him away now.

His fingers release the buttons of my dress in seconds and then they go to work on my jeans, undoing them and pulling them free of my legs in one sweep. I am clad in nothing but a light dress and my panties.

"Since I've met you, I've thought about nothing but fucking you," he says, pulling my dress over my head.

The words bring another lightning bolt of lust sweeping through me. I can't resist him.

With my bra exposed, he slides his fingers over and around my breasts, kneading them with his hands.

I gasp under the pressure. His grip is strong, almost painful. I can feel his erection pushing against me.

Then he pulls away my panties and tosses them free of the bed.

A whirlwind of feelings are hammering through my heart and body. There's a deep shame of lying on his bed, naked from the waist down.

But there's another knowledge too. I want this. For the first time in what feels like forever, I really want this.

He forces a knee between my legs and kicks them apart. Then he slides his thumb in between my legs, running it over and around my clitoris.

"You're so wet," he murmurs appreciatively. "I'm going to fuck you so hard."

"Please," I beg, "wait." The realisation of what is about to happen is hitting home.

He stops, his face confused although his erection, hard against my thigh, knows exactly what it wants.

"You don't want me to go hard?"

"I'm not very experienced," I admit, blushing at the confession.

Suddenly, he's sat up.

"What do you mean by not very experienced?"

Damn. Why didn't I copy Lorna and spend my graduation year having one-night stands?

"I've only had sex with one person," I say, adding, "at least I think we had sex."

"You *think* you had sex?" his voice is incredulous, but there's a kindness, a concern.

He pulls away a little, so he's no longer pinning me down.

"I dated my male friend," I say, mortified that he's extracting the admission of inexperience from me. Just once in my life, I wish the seductress which people keep casting me as was really true.

My body is still coursing with desire for him.

"We tried," I said, the memory of Jerome's and my fumblings coming back in lurid detail, "but it was painful. I'm not sure if I had sex or not."

"I see." He lets his hand run down the length of my body, considering.

"Do you want to have sex now?"

What a thing to ask!

I look down at my naval. Surely that must be obvious.

"I might read that expression to mean that you do."

I want him so badly, it must be written in every part of my body.

His hand slides down again between my legs, and I pull in a quick intake of breath.

"Certainly it feels like you want to have sex," he considers, and his fingers begin a tantalising, delicious dance over my clitoris.

The sensation is so powerful, it's almost unbearable. I feel a dark, deep heat rising up, spreading up my thighs.

"Has anyone ever made you come before?" He asks this gently, his fingers continuing their silky sliding movement.

The feeling is building, building. I feel as though I'm about to explode.

"No," I gasp.

"Have you made yourself come?"

"Yes," I manage. I would tell him anything, right at this moment. Anything he asked.

"Good. Later you will show me."

Show him? How I touch myself? Even his suggesting it makes me want to die of shame.

"I am not so much of a brute that I would fuck you now, Isabella, after that admission. But the thought of giving you your first orgasm. I can't help myself. You are so very appealing, lying there."

He shifts his hand slightly, thrusting his fingers inside me. I breathe in sharply. The sensation is different. Deeper. Rougher.

"You are small," he says, looking into my eyes. "That is why you have found sex painful. But we can stretch you a little, to accommodate."

He's looking into my eyes as if asking permission. I nod, hardly able to do anything else.

He pushes his hand faster, building up a rhythm, in and out, with his thumb sliding over my clitoris. I gasp. The feeling of him moving inside me hurts, but only a little. And the light movements of his thumb are exquisite.

The combined sensations are more than I can bear.

It feels as though he is stretching me open. His fingers shift a little and begin thrusting hard into an unbelievably pleasurable place inside me.

"That's your G-spot," he murmurs, looking into my eyes and pushing again. Then he moves his thumb again, sliding it fast over my clitoris.

Pleasure and pain have mingled in one, and his hand forces me wider and his fingers work on my clitoris.

The heat builds up until it explodes in a rain of golden light, coursing warmly through my entire body.

I arch my back and gasp as the pleasure rolls over me.

And then the heat subsides and I'm lying, gasping on his bed, reeling the sweet aftershock.

Berkeley raises his hand to his mouth, and sucks his fingers.

"You taste delicious," he says, "and you look unbelievably sexy in the throws of orgasm."

I stare up at him, aware that my cheeks are flushed and I am panting.

He looks confused suddenly.

"I didn't realise you were such an innocent," he says, almost to himself. "Words can't describe how much I want to fuck you at this moment, Isabella."

He looks torn.

What the hell? One minute he's taking my orgasm to another level and the next he's saying he doesn't want to have sex with me?

"Have dinner with me," he says suddenly.

"What?" I sit up on the bed, more confused than I've ever been in my life.

"Stay," he says. "Have dinner with me here. I'll order in whatever you like. We'll talk about the screen test."

"What else will we talk about?"

"What do you mean?" he looks surprised.

"I mean, are we going to talk about what the hell is going on?" I say. My temper is rising. "You tell me we shouldn't have a relationship. Then you tell me you do. Then you give me the best orgasm of my life, and then you say you won't have sex with me?"

He looks apologetic. "I'm sorry, Isabella," he says. "I've never been in this situation before. You've taken me by surprise. And the last thing I want to do is hurt you."

Hurt me. Is this a goodbye speech?

"But I don't want you to get involved with me without knowing what you're letting yourself in for."

"What are you talking about?"

"Today…" he stops, runs his fingers through his brown hair, and then peers up at me through his green eyes. "It has been so long before I've felt what I felt today."

Is he talking about love? Lust?

"Sex isn't usually like that for me," he says. "I don't usually find myself able to engage in the way we've just experienced."

Lust then. I knew it.

"You have to understand," he says, "that if we are to see more of each other, it might not be on terms you find agreeable."

"What do you mean?"

"I mean sexually, Isabella. You are very different to the usual person I relate to sexually. You have something… unique. But I am an old-fashioned man."

He sighs and his face looks older, suddenly, and world-weary.

"What do you mean?" I am staring at him. *Old-fashioned?*

"My sex life and the way I work are very closely related, Isabella."

"But I thought you didn't get involved with actresses?"

"I don't. But the way I relate in my sex life is the same as the way I produce and direct. I require obedience, at all times."

Obedience? What does he mean?

"What sort of obedience?" I manage.

His mouth sets in a hard serious line.

"Total obedience."

Chapter 10

Total obedience? My mouth is dry, and suddenly his enormous bedroom feels unbelievably small.

"Let me fix you dinner," he says, and his eyes are soft, conciliatory. "And I can explain things better."

He offers a hand to pull me up off the bed, and I take it, feeling powerless to resist. I realise suddenly I'm sat on his bed wearing only my bra, and my face begins to burn.

"Go out of the room," I mumble, "and let me get dressed."

Berkeley gives an easy laugh.

"Ok," he says, getting up. "Though there's no reason for you to be modest. There's nothing you have to be ashamed of."

He gives my naked body a meaningful stare, and I squirm under his gaze, crossing my legs.

"Fine!" he puts his hands up in the air in a gesture of surrender. "I'll go out and work out what's best to order for dinner."

I'm shaking my head. It's all become too much suddenly. I can't deal with all these feelings. I need to be away from him.

"I need to go," I say, throwing on my clothes.

"Really?" As he says the words, I realise I am only half sure of them.

"I need to know what's happening," I say.

"It's complicated." He looks haunted.

I sigh, pushing my hair off my face. "I'm not sure I can do complicated," I say. And I mean it. These last few days have been the most exciting and the most tiring of my entire life. I'm not sure I have the energy for any more James Berkeley.

He moves towards me, and just his proximity is like fire running through my nerves. Then he gently pulls me to my feet and leads me back into his enormous lounge.

"Please, Isabella." He tilts my chin up so my eyes meet his. "Stay with me," he whispers. "Just for a few hours. So we can talk."

Talk. Right. After what just happened in the bedroom. But a man offering to talk has to be a rarity.

I stare back at him, not sure how to answer.

"You are mesmerising," he says, staring into my eyes, "on and off camera."

I smile, blush, and tug my chin free of his hand.

"So you'll stay?" he asks.

I nod, not trusting myself to speak.

"I'll fix us something to eat. Make yourself comfortable."

He gestures to the open lounge, filled with beautiful designer furniture. Night has closed on now, and the huge glass windows show a sweeping panoramic of the dramatically floodlit St Pauls Cathedral, and the Southbank.

I eye the furniture uncertainly. It may look beautiful, but it sure as hell doesn't look comfortable. It's hard to pick out a single piece which even looks like it could be sat on. A woman's touch, I think, is much needed.

I choose a chesterfield-style chaise lounge which has been finished in thick faun covered leather and take a seat.

James vanishes into the studio room, and I hear a muted conversation on his telephone.

Then he returns.

"I've asked my driver to pick us up a selection of food from Harrods' Food Hall," he says. "I trust that will meet with your tastes."

I nod. I've only ever been to Harrods once, and that was as a wide-eyed window shopper. The food hall is piled high with the most incredible fresh produce and handmade dishes prepared by London's best chefs. I remember seeing a TV presenter buying a prepared side of beef for £200.

"In the meantime, perhaps we might have a glass of Champagne?" he adds, "to celebrate your success today?"

"My success?"

"Behind the camera."

I blush and look down.

"Don't be embarrassed, Isabella," he says, moving across the room, and seating himself next to me on the chaise lounge. This close I can feel his body heat.

"It's just that I don't think I'm cut out for a movie role," I say. "I was only ever considering theatre. And even that was to make me better educated as a script writer."

"In my experience, there are two kinds of actors," says James. "There are the actors like Marilyn Monroe who everybody recognises. They are charismatic and compelling, and they play the same character over and over. There are plenty of those actors around and they get all the major movie parts."

He leans in a little closer and meets me eyes.

"Then there are the actors who really become the thing they act. Those people are team-players. They work with everybody else to bring a performance together. And they are humble. Because they don't mind that they are not recognised when they play different parts. All they want is to make the act real."

I nod. That makes sense.

"You are the second kind, Isabella, and a very rare and special kind you are."

I give him a shy smile. I had never thought of it that way before. But now I consider it, he's right. Most of the students at drama school wanted to be big names. When they acted, it was all about them. I don't act that way. But it never occurred to me that could be a good thing.

"Thank you," I say.

"You should know that behind the camera you are the sexiest and most fuckable thing I have seen in my entire life," he says. "It's all I can do not to rip those clothes off you again right now and have you on this couch."

I blush. *How can he say these things?*

"Champagne." He says, his voice changing as he stands up.

"I don't drink."

"Do you have a physical difficulty with alcohol?"

I shake my head.

The tone in his voice changes. "Did something happen to you?"

I nod, and for some reason tears come into my eyes. I blink them away, furious with myself.

"What happened?" asks James. "Can you tell me?" His voice is full of concern. He sits back on the chaise lounge and takes my hand.

For some reason this makes it easier to tell him the truth.

"I had my drink spiked," I say. "In a bar on Trafalgar Square. I was there at a party with my friend Lorna. Someone must have put something in my drink. I had a few sips and before I knew it, I could hardly stand."

I close my eyes for a moment, remembering the dreadful frightening feeling of my legs going out from under me.

He nods, looking grave.

"Then someone grabbed me," I continue, "and tried to drag me out of the club." The horrible mental picture flashes back. The hands under my armpits. The sense of powerlessness as my limp body offered no resistance.

His eyes are on mine, his hand squeezes my fingers. I notice his free hand is balled into a fist and the knuckles are white.

"What happened next?" he asks. His voice is tight.

"He didn't manage to get me outside," I say. "Someone must have stopped him, or he must have got spooked. The bouncers found me in the entrance hall."

Berkeley lets out a breath, and I realise that until that moment he had been holding every muscle in his body tense.

"Isabella." He stops and for a moment, I think he is lost for words. "I don't know what is happening between us," he says. "I hope at the very least you will agree to share your talent in the role I have in mind for you." He stops again, squeezing my hand.

"But whatever happens, I will never let any harm come to you, do you understand that?" He's staring fiercely into my eyes, and the intensity in them is frightening. "Nothing or no one will ever hurt you, Isabella, so long as it is in my power to prevent it."

It's strange, but I really believe him. And it feels like a relief.

"But you must put your faith in me and trust I have your best interests at heart," he continues.

I nod again, wondering what just happened. Did James Berkeley just make a pledge to always protect me? I feel like a fairy tale heroine.

"And today it is in your best interests to drink a glass of Champagne with me," he says with a sudden boyish grin. His lighter mood is infectious and I grin back. He looks his real youthful age suddenly, and I wonder how often this younger Berkeley has a chance to shine.

He bounds to his feet and, in a moment, is opening a large refrigerator which is tastefully secreted away behind one of the ultra-modern kitchen cabinet doors.

"There are two ways of drinking alcohol," he explains as he pulls free a golden bottle of Champagne and two iced flutes with a flourish.

"One is to drink for the sake of getting drunk. The other is to savour only the finest available, as one of life's pleasures. I indulge in the latter."

His strong fingers ease out the cork with a loud *pop* and he tilts the glasses and lets the golden liquid flow.

"I think you will like working on a movie-set Isabella," he says, returning to my side of the room and handing me a glass.

I take a sip of the chilled liquid. The fizz is intoxicating. I smile up at him. But I am not so sure I agree about the movie-set thing.

The doorbell sounds, and he pads over in his bare feet and jeans to answer it. I can't hear the exchange, but he returns with two beautiful wicker hampers tied with cloth and ribbon.

"I thought we might enjoy a little urban picnic," he says, his eyes twinkling.

"Sounds like a great idea," I say, feeling suddenly hungry.

With the views across the Thames and the lights of London, I can hardly think of a more romantic evening.

Carefully, James unpacks the hampers and lays out plates of food.

There is fresh bread, cheeses, a whole chicken, hand-made pasta, smoked salmon and caviar.

"That's a lot of food," I say, as he removes a tiny jar filled with oil.

"Have you had white truffles before?" he asks.

"No."

"They're not to everyone's taste, but I think you are sophisticated enough to enjoy them," he says. He's grinning, so I have to assume he's joking.

"Here." He uncorks the jar and a delicious aroma fills the air. "Can you smell that?"

He holds the jar towards me and I nod.

"Do you like it?"

"Yes. It's incredible," I say.

"Sexy isn't it?" he says, grinning, and I grin back at him. It's true, it is a sexy kind of smell. Powerful and intense.

James prepares a plate with the fresh pasta and shaves truffle over the top. Then he carves up the chicken and adds that to the plate.

"Wine," he decides, getting to his feet again and returning to his vast kitchen space. He selects a bottle from outside the fridge this time and returns with two large crystal wine glasses.

"White is usually the choice for pasta, but the intensity of this can take a red," he says, uncorking and pouring. "And besides, I have this bottle I wanted to share with you, so we may cheat a little on wine etiquette."

I take a forkful of pasta and the truffle explodes in my mouth.

"Try it with some wine," he says, smiling appreciatively at my enjoyment. I try a sip and the combination is mind-blowing.

"This is so good," I say, closing my eyes as the heavenly flavours combine.

I gaze out over the river.

"Is this your standard seduction technique?" I tease.

To my surprise, he looks thoughtful.

"I've never made a woman a picnic in my apartment, no," he says, almost regretfully.

"But you've had plenty women back here, I imagine," I say, pushing another forkful of pasta into my mouth. The taste is just amazing.

He shakes his head. "The women that I've been involved with would have to pass certain tests of obedience before they would be allowed in here."

I almost choke on a mouthful of pasta. I stare at him, trying to work out if he's serious.

"Isabella, do you know why I didn't have sex with you just now, in my bedroom?" he asks.

I shake my head, a forkful of food halfway to my mouth, trying to work out where this is headed.

He sighs, and runs his fingers through his hair.

"I didn't have sex with you because you don't have a great deal of experience," he says.

I try not to look offended.

"That's not a bad thing," he adds. "It's just very different to what I'm used to."

He is staring steadily into my eyes.

"I have never wanted to fuck anyone as much as I want to fuck you," he says.

I swallow. *Oh.*

"But in my relationships, I am the man and the woman is the woman."

Ok. So he's some old-fashioned guy. But I knew that. Didn't I?

"That means that I also wield the power to exercise discipline."

Discipline? I think back to the rumours about him on set. The controlling nature. Dictating who his actresses date.

"Is this related to how you work?" I ask.

He shakes his head. "This is something different entirely. Which is why I do not form relationships with my actresses."

He takes a sip of wine. Something in his eyes has changed. As though he is assessing me.

"Do you remember when you first acted Juliet for me?" he says.

I nod, taking a sip of wine. I need it.

"That is how I would have you in our relationship," he says.

My eyes widen. "You want me to plead with you? To beg you?"

"There would be times when you would need to beg me, yes," he says, choosing his words carefully. "But I more refer to the wider context of that relationship. Juliet is submissive to Lord Capulet's will. She is his to do what he wants with."

What?

"But Juliet doesn't do exactly what Lord Capulet wants," I counter, feeling all at sea in the conversation. I have no idea what he's talking about. "She pleads with him, but she's also contradicting his will."

"Very well-observed," says James. "In our relationship, you would be mine to do what I will with. And if you defied me, I would punish you. Discipline you."

Discipline me?

"What do you mean by discipline?" I whisper. My mouth is dry and my heart is beating fast. *What is he suggesting?*

"Physically discipline you," he says. "In a manner in which I see fit."

"What if I don't want to be disciplined?" I say.

"Then you have every right to refuse," says James. His voice sounds casual, as though he's scheduling an office meeting. "But I think a relationship between us might be difficult."

He looks apologetic for a moment. Then he sighs.

"Something in you, Isabella, makes me gentle. Gentler than I have ever been. But I think it is too late to change the man I am. I don't deny that I want you. But it must be on my terms."

"What do you mean by physical discipline?" I ask, wondering how deranged this conversation can get.

"A manner in which I see fit," he repeats.

"Explain to me an example," I demand flatly.

His eyes flick to mine, assessing, testing.

"Your lateness," he says.

"Yes." I'm not sure I like how this is going.

"Lateness is a sign of disobedience," he says. "That first time I had come to collect you in the car. I was exercising courtesy. You were late. That was discourteous."

"I… I'm sorry," I say, uncertainly. It's true that lateness is a bad habit of mine. I'd never thought of it as impolite.

"Do you know how much I wanted to pull down your panties and give you a good spanking in that car?" he says.

Oh.

I flush crimson. But there's another feeling too. I can't deny it. His words arouse me.

"That," he says, "is what I mean by discipline." And he places a forkful of food in his mouth.

I find myself standing up. I feel dizzy, confused. It's all coming to me at once. *I like this guy. More than I've ever liked anyone. And he wants to turn me into some medieval female stereotype.*

"I wouldn't share this with you," adds James, "if I did not see something in you which wants to comply to my wishes."

Something in me? Sure I'm quiet and I let people boss me around. But do I want to be spanked for showing up a few minutes late? It's all so confusing.

"I… I need to think," I say, not wanting to admit how tantalising the prospect of spending more time with him is.

"Sit down, Isabella," he says, "and finish your wine."

The tone in his voice has an almost physical effect on my knee joints, and I buckle, sitting back down on the floor.

This confuses me even more. Do I want this? This man telling me what to do?

"I have never felt the way about anyone that I feel about you," he says softly. "And if you decide you can't have a relationship with me, then I understand. I will still cast you and do my best to bring out the best in you. Although," he adds, his green eyes darkening, "it will take all my physical control to see you through that camera and not take you on the studio floor once we finish filming."

I flush and force myself to stand, still holding the wine glass. I need to retain some semblance of control.

"I need to think things over," I say, taking a nervous sip.

"That's exactly what I want you to do," he says, eyeing me from his position on the floor. Something about his stance reminds me of a tiger about to pounce.

I let my eyes roam around the flat, anxious for some distraction from the intensity of our conversation.

Was it the English boarding school which did this to him? I wonder. It's common knowledge that the masters still cane the boys at school.

"I need to know more," I decide. "I need to know more about why you want this from me."

His face takes on a troubled look.

"Was it your school?" I press, "Were you beaten as a boy?"

"I was beaten as a boy," he says, "but that is nothing to do with why I want your obedience. Almost the opposite, in fact," he adds, more to himself than to me.

"What do you mean?"

His eyes lock with mine. "Isabella, my past is my business, and if you continue to press me then I really will put you over my knee and give you a spanking, whether you've agreed to it or not."

I flush.

"Have all your other girlfriends agreed to this?" I ask.

"Only one," he says.

Only one?

"After her, there were no other girlfriends," he adds, "only sexual liaisons."

Oh. So he's telling me there was some great love of his life, and she let him beat her.

"Why did you split up?" I say, hoping this doesn't count as the kind of enquiry which merits physical discipline.

"We didn't," he says shortly. "She died. Of a drug overdose."

The look of pain in his face is so acute that I can't stand it.

I move back over to where he's sitting and seat myself beside him.

"I'm sorry," I say, taking his hand. "I truly am."

He looks at me distractedly. Suddenly, I catch a glimpse of something. Is this demand for obedience his way of salving some great pain deep inside?

Can I agree to it? Could I be helping him?

"I'll think about it," I say, and I see relief light his features. "But you have to do something for me."

"What?"

"You say you are gentler around me."

His features soften. "Yes."

"Perhaps you could try and find out what it is that makes you gentler, so you can practise it more."

He nods, looking down at the floor with a little smile. Then he meets my eyes.

"I'm going to let you go now, Isabella, so you can think things over. And believe me, nothing is quite so exquisitely painful as watching you leave."

He pauses for a moment and I realise he must have felt this on another occasion. Maybe even more than one. Was it as painful for him to leave me at the restaurant earlier than it was for me? Certainly he looked hurt when I left him in his suite last night.

"But you must grant me permission to take you out tomorrow night, so that I might persuade you to my way of thinking."

I'm not sure how I feel about being persuaded.

"You don't need to be anxious," he adds. "I am not taking you anywhere that you couldn't tell your mother about."

My mother. Right. Like I would tell her I'm on a date with a man who wants to spank me for showing up late.

"But it is a surprise. That is part of the deal. I am in charge." He gives a devilish grin.

I sigh. Can I accept this?

"Somewhere I can tell me mother about?" I venture.

"Yes."

That doesn't sound too bad.

"Ok," I accept warily.

"Good. The car will collect you at 8pm. Make sure you've had something to eat."

Not dinner then. I mentally cross that option off the list. Then what?

He stands up, pulling me up with him by the hands.

"Now," he says, "before you go, I am going to give you something to remember me by."

He sweeps me into his arms, and his mouth is like fire, his tongue moving sensually, and his lips bringing alive every sense in my body.

Wow.

Then he reaches his hand down and strikes my behind in a sharp little spank. I gasp as a surge of desire runs through me.

"Now go, and think about what I said," he whispers as he releases me. And I realise with a sense of foreboding that I don't know how I will be able to resist this dangerous man doing anything he wants with me.

Chapter 11

Click. The lens shutter hammers away as Chris angles the camera.

"Beautiful! Beautiful, Isabella."

He drops to his knees, angling the camera up under my face.

"Just a few more."

I'm dressed like a medieval princess, with a long flowing dress and a small crown. My black hair flows beneath it, and I wear a heavy piece of gold-coloured costume jewellery at my neck.

"Lovely." Chris moves around to the other side, clicking away.

My slightly bizarre part-time job came courtesy of Lorna, who introduced me to Chris at a party. Chris is a classic London cockney photographer who started out snapping glamour girls and celebrities.

He's since expanded to supply book covers and portrait shots, but can always be relied upon to supply the latest celebrity gossip.

"Come on, Isabella," he says, unleashing a flurry of shutter shots, "give me that reluctant model look I love."

I'm a terrible model, but for some reason my face just fits for a series of historical romance books. Chris roped me into the job a year ago, when he found that model agencies couldn't supply him with a girl who looked medieval enough.

I also look a lot more ordinary than girls like Lorna, who would look too modern and model-like decked out in olden day costumes, so I got the gig. And it earns me a few hundred pounds every six months or so when a new title is released.

"Ok," says Chris, "just a few more."

The shutter clicks again, and then he puts the camera down.

"Perfect."

I give a sigh of relief. Standing in the heavy dress for hours is exhausting.

"Here." Chris throws me my phone. "You have about a hundred missed calls on this."

I catch the phone – no easy job in princess robes – and check the screen.

Ten missed calls flash up at me and four messages.

I scan through them. All from James Berkeley. *What the hell?*

My immediate thought is he must be phoning to cancel, and my heart drops a little.

I scroll through the texts.

Need to talk to you about tonight.

Isabella, call me.

Are you alright?

Call me. I'm worried.

Wow. The guy is determined. Maybe that's what makes famous directors. I click to call him back, mentally revising my evening. Lorna's out partying as usual, so maybe I'll have a much-deserved quiet night in.

The phone picks up after one ring.

"Isabella, are you alright?"

The intensity of his answer throws me.

"Yes. Yes I'm fine."

I hear him sigh in relief.

"I thought something might have happened to you."

"Nothing bad can happen to me with you around, remember," I tease.

I look over the room to see Chris staring at me. With my poor dating history, he's not used to hearing me flirt on the phone.

"But I'm not with you," growls James. "That's the problem." He lets out a little huff of air. "Where are you?"

"I'm in a photography studio."

"You're *where*?"

A feeling of uneasiness creeps through me. Something tells me Mr-Old-Fashioned is not going to like another man taking my picture.

"I have a part-time job having my picture taken for historic book covers," I explain.

"Who is taking the photos?" His voice is icy.

"A photographer," I snap back.

"Answer the question, Isabella," he says, and there's a dangerous tone in his voice.

Have I made him angry?

The idea has a new dimension now he's said what he'd like to do to me if I step out of line.

"Chris," I say carefully. "He's a celebrity photographer who shoots book covers."

There's a silence as he considers this.

"Isabella, I don't like men taking photos of you," he says.

Surprise, surprise.

"But since we haven't yet reached a mutual agreement as to how we might progress, I will have to contain my annoyance."

I'm not sure how to respond, so I change the subject. "Why did you call?" I ask.

"I needed to give you some information about this evening. About what to wear."

Oh. So we are still on. But he's starting with the obsessive dressing me thing again.

"I want you wearing a dress," he says, "something feminine and not too short."

Excuse me?

"Listen," I say, my hackles rising. "As you so correctly stated before, we haven't reached an arrangement. You are not going to dictate to me what to wear."

Chris has stopped packing away his camera and is looking at me in amazement.

"It's important," says James, his voice softening. "Trust me, Isabella. It's not about my dictating to you. It impacts on where we're going this evening. Believe me, it would be very remiss for me not to explain what you needed to wear."

Possibilities and questions are rising up in my mind. What on earth could we be doing that requires such a specific outfit? Surely, he's just using it as an excuse?

"Alright," I say slowly. "I'll wear what you suggest. But if I get there and find it's not necessary, then you'll be in big trouble."

He gives a soft laugh. "Believe me, Isabella," he says. "When I'm around you, I'm always in trouble."

There's a click and the line goes dead. I'm left standing in my princess dress with Chris gaping at me.

"Who was *that?*" he manages. "Someone has finally managed to get through to that cold heart of yours?"

Chris is joking. He's a massive flirt and makes no secret of the fact he'd like to have sex with me. But seeing as he does this with every girl on the planet, I don't take it personally.

"Shut up, Chris." I am grinning.

"Oh my God!"

"It's not like that." I'm shaking my head.

"Ohhhhh. So what is it like then?"

You tell me. I've found a man who wants to turn back the equality clock about two hundred years.

"It's complicated," I say.

"They're all complicated, darlin'" says Chris, shouldering his bag. "And right now, *I* am about to join several of you gorgeous complicated female creatures in the boozer down the road for a pint. Care to join us?"

I laugh. "No thanks, Chris."

"Fair enough."

"You make sure this geezer treats you right," he adds, making his way out of the studio and leaving me to change and lock up. "You're a special girl, Isabella, you need to be treated special."

Oh, he wants to treat me special alright.

"Bye, Chris." I give him a tired wave, wondering what life must be like in his easy world of flirting and sex. "I'll keep that in mind."

Chapter 12

Lorna is buzzing round me excitedly as I dress for my date.

I've chosen a green dress with a fitted fifties style halter-top and a flowing skirt. And since his gift of the Jimmy Choos are the only genuine designer shoes I own, I've reluctantly slipped them on. James Berkeley has a habit of choosing fancy locations, and I don't want to look out of place.

"A secret date!" says Lorna. "How romantic is that?"

I have a feeling she wouldn't think it was quite so romantic if she knew the reasoning behind it.

So that I might persuade you to my way of thinking.

The thought gives me a thrill of fear. He also promised it would be something I could explain to my mother. How bad could it be?

There's a ring of the doorbell as I'm making the final touches to my make-up.

Lorna looks at me knowingly.

"That'll be him!"

"I don't think so, Lorna. Last time he waited in the car. Besides," I check my watch. "It's only a quarter to eight."

I return to fixing my hair to match the dress. I've chosen to sweep it up into a chignon, but right now it's misbehaving.

I hear Lorna answer the door and then a male voice. My heart skips a beat.

Then he's there, in my doorway, looking beyond handsome in a grey wool coat, and holding an elegantly wrapped bunch of yellow roses.

Lorna is behind him, almost bouncing up and down with glee.

"She's in here, Mr Berkeley," she says, her eyes glued to his face. Over the past few days, I've conveniently forgotten that every other female on the planet finds James Berkeley irresistible. Why did I ever think he might be interested in me?

A wave of depression sweeps over me.

I'm just another sexual liaison to him, I think, remembering his words. The love of his life is dead. I wonder at how beautiful she must have been to make him fall in love with her.

Lorna melts away into the hallway, and suddenly there's only me and him, standing in my bedroom.

"Very nice," he says, looking around the room.

"Oh." I glance around distractedly. My room is a homely jumble of flea-market finds, and furnishings from the nearby Portobello Market.

"It's just things I've collected over the years."

"I was talking about you," he murmurs, taking a step closer and handing me the flowers. His eyes follow the halter-neck of my green dress.

"Thank you." I take them from him. I've never had such a beautiful bouquet. The green paper wrapping is emblazoned with the words Orlando Hamilton. I recognise the name from the newspapers. This is the florist which Guy Ritchie used to send flowers to Madonna.

"They're a clue to where we're going tonight," he says.

I frown. This doesn't help at all. Unless we're going to a flower show. Unlikely.

"They're also yellow rather than red," he says. "Do you know what that signifies?"

I shake my head.

"Jealousy," he says.

What? My eyes widen in surprise.

"I do not like you being photographed by other men, Isabella," he says. "If we come to an arrangement between us, behaviour of that sort will command a very heavy kind of punishment."

I place the flowers on my dressing table.

"But we haven't reached an arrangement," I remind him, smiling sweetly.

Ha.

He smiles infuriatingly.

"We'll see." He looks around the bedroom and his gaze falls on my bed. I feel the heat rising in my cheeks.

It's a large sleigh-bed which I got for a steal in an auction, and as an item of furniture it's my pride and joy. But the way Berkeley is looking at it is giving my favourite purchase a whole new meaning.

"It's shame there's no place I can tie you to that bed," he says.

He wants to tie me to my bed?

The thought is outrageous and sexy at the same time.

He steps closer and runs his hand under my chin.

"But first I have something arranged for you."

"Aren't you going to tell me what it is now?" My voice comes out as a squeak. The bed remark has made me flustered despite my best intentions to play it cool.

"Not yet." He smiles, and the boyish carefree James who I caught a glimpse of last night returns.

"Come with me," he leans forward to plunk a single yellow rose from the bouquet, and then offers me his arm.

We pass Lorna in the hallway and she waves us out. I pray she hasn't been listening in on Berkeley's pillow talk.

She frowns at me as we leave, and I realise she's signalling me to be safe. For whatever reason, she doesn't trust Berkeley.

I roll my eyes and mouth 'OK' back at her, and then we're out of the apartment.

As we slide into the backseat of the car Berkeley reaches into his pocket and presents me with a slim wrapped box. He still holds the single yellow rose in his other hand.

"What's this," I ask, as the car pulls away, "another gift?"

"In a manner of speaking." His eyes twitch in amusement. "Although it's more a gift for me."

I tear off the paper, looking at him questioningly. Under the wrapping is a card box. I ease of the lid, and inside is a silk blindfold.

"You'll need to wear it," he says.

I stare at him.

"Isabella," he says gently. "Trust me."

He takes it from my hands and eases it over my eyes. The silk is soft on my face.

"It's so you can't see where we're going," he explains.

From behind the dark of the mask, the world has taken on another hue. And it's filled with James Berkeley. The heat of his body, the scent of his skin. I realise suddenly that every cell in my body is heightened, crying out for him to touch me.

Did he know it would have this effect?

"Is this how you take all your dates out?" I ask in a poor attempt at humour.

He doesn't laugh.

"The back of this car has been made to certain requirements," he says. "The driver can't hear or see us from the front unless I press a switch enabling it."

He's silent for a moment, allowing this information to sink in.

"Have you had a lot of women in here?" I can't help myself; the jealous memory of Lorna and all the other girls who must fall over him has risen to the fore.

"Yes," he says, and there's humour in his voice. "I have fucked women in the back of this car. You are the only woman I have taken blindfold in it."

"Oh." I chew at my lip nervously, wondering what my face looks like half-covered with the blindfold.

Suddenly James's mouth is at my ear, blowing gently.

"Words cannot explain what an effect you're having on me, blindfolded like that," he says.

A wonderful fragrance fills the air near my nostrils, and I realise he must be holding the rose close to my face. Then the soft petals touch my forehead and sweep slowly down my face.

My lips part slightly as the bloom runs gently over them. And then James sweeps the rose slowly downwards, across my collar bones and then down to where my green halter-dress meets the tops of my breasts.

Wherever it touches seems to make my skin hypersensitive.

"Tonight, I am going to teach you what it means to be obedient to me," he murmurs, as the petals touch where my breasts meet.

I gasp as he dallies with the flower over the sensitive skin. Every cell in my body is yearning for him, for his touch.

His hand is on my thigh. I tense and then relax.

"I'm going to make you come now," he whispers, stroking his hand slowly upwards, so it slides beneath my skirt. "I've been thinking about it since you left last night. I want to touch you. Would you like that?"

"Yes," I whisper. There's no point in lying. Desire is coming off me in waves. It feels as though every part of my skin is extra sensitive.

"Good." The hand moves higher. "Open your legs."

I part my thighs a little, and he plunges his hand between them, pulling them forcibly apart. I gasp.

"You needn't be anxious, Isabella," he says. "No one can see us, and you haven't given me permission to inflict any pain on you."

He works his hand higher, gently trailing his fingers along the inside of my thigh. "And as you can see, Isabella, you bring out a gentle side to me."

My thighs tense at his touch.

"Do you want me to stop?" He whispers it dangerously. I shake my head.

"Say it," he commands.

I shake my head again. "No," I whisper, "I don't want you to stop."

As his fingers reach the apex of my thighs, I almost cry out loud.

"You're so wet," he murmurs. "I'm looking forward to fucking you later."

His fingers slide in and out of me.

"Turn around," he says, "and lie on your front."

I hesitate, uncertain of what he wants from me. And then he takes me by the hips and turns me so I am lying face down on the leather seat of the car, with my legs parted either side of him.

"I'm not going to fuck you now," he murmurs. "But since I'm about to afford you pleasure, I think it's only fair that you give me a view to make it worth my while."

He pushes up my skirt, and then tugs at my hips, pulling me so my rear is lifted off the seat.

"Very nice," he says, tugging down my panties.

I feel a confusing mix of excitement and shame course through me. Facing down with my naked behind waving upwards is thrilling and embarrassing at the same time.

Then I feel his fingers slide in between my legs and up over my clitoris, and all thoughts of embarrassment leave me. With the blindfold closing off my vision, the sensation is heightened everywhere. And as he strokes his fingers, faster and faster over my wetness, I feel the orgasm build.

With his other hand he plunges inside me, and the combination of two movements is too much to bear. I tumble over the edge, letting out a deep moan of pleasure as he thrusts at me faster and deeper.

I collapse forward on my belly, panting.

"So quickly," he says admiringly. "I like that I can have such an effect on you."

He pulls me around and upright again, breaking me out of my post-orgasmic bliss. My hands move to my blind-fold. I want to kiss him, to reciprocate in some way, but he gently restrains my hands.

"We're nearly at our destination," he says. "Better you stay in a presentable state in case there are any paparazzi.

Paparazzi? Where is he taking me?

He slides up my panties and I wriggle gratefully back into them, wishing I had a spare pair.

"I hope this evening changes your mind," he says, "because if I don't fuck you later tonight, I'm going to explode."

I've been wondering about that myself. Even for a man of Berkeley's obvious self-control, it seems a lot to ask that he stay celibate whilst bringing me to orgasm.

The car veers to the side, then slows and stops. My heart begins pounding out of my chest. *Where the hell is he taking me?*

His strong fingers tug off the blindfold, and I am greeted with the welcome view of his perfect features staring down at me.

He looks amused as I blink up at him.

From behind the tinted windows I can't see anything much. A London street with more warehouse type buildings. Are we back at his apartment?

"We're in Shoreditch," he says to my unasked question. "Can you guess why we're here?"

I shake my head.

"I'll give you another clue," he says, reaching under the seat. "I realise you have raised an objection to my buying you clothes, but these, I'm afraid Isabella, are a necessity.

He tugs out a shoebox and opens the lid. Inside is a pair of beautiful handmade shoes. They have a low heel and are made from deep red satin.

Wonderingly, I take them out.

They look like… dancing shoes.

"We're going dancing?" I guess.

His face breaks into a smile. "I am taking you to the *La Catedral de Tango*," he says, his voice rolling expertly over the Spanish words. "And you will understand what it means to be an obedient partner."

Chapter 13

The *Catedral de Tango* is a large building in the London Regency style, with a grand entrance of Greek columns. But rather than the glitzy frontages of London's west end buildings, the *Catedral* looks a little scuffed and work-in. We enter a black marble lobby, which has been decorated with works from local artists.

A modern sculpture depicts two tango dancers in an abstract way, and pictures on the wall are cartoon sketches and works of graffiti. The combined effect is young, contemporary and boutique.

"This is a part of London the tourists don't get to see," says James with a gleam in his eye. "The artist's quarter and the music scene. It's hidden. Only known to a few."

James pays our way in, handing a banknote to the punk-looking girl taking money, and leads me into the main room, still clutching my shoes.

"You can leave your footwear there," he says, pointing to a large shoe rack which has been artfully wrought from old bicycle parts.

I lean on his arm, removing my heels and taking in the room before us.

It is only half-lit, with enormous ceilings leading up to a huge chandelier fashioned from car hub caps.

Towards the back are a few large tables which obviously provide the bar. They are lined with chic-looking bottles of spirits.

In the main body of the room is a huge circuit, and parading around and through it are hundreds of young tango dancers. They are dressed in a mixture of indy clothing, vintage and classic tango dresses and suits. And they whirl around the room at their own pace. Some are slower, still getting the feel for the dance. Others are expert, and dance at a dizzying pace, the men tumbling the girls so they sweep inches from the floor. As my eyes follow the edge of the group, a beautiful girl in a green dress is held low by her partner. Her whole body slows, and her leg sweeps a large elegant tango circle outwards against the floor.

Then her partner rights her, stepping her back in time to the music, and they dance away in dizzying perfection.

"You took dance at college?"

James mouth is by my ear, and I'm jerked out of my fascinated study of the dancers.

"Yes," I say, still mesmerised by the scene. The couples are so beautiful.

"But not Tango?" he guesses.

I shake my head and return to exchanging my shoes for the lovely hand-made pair he's given me.

Fumbling, I tighten the straps. My feet now look perfect for Tango dancing. It's the rest of me I have to worry about.

I straighten up and find myself locked against James, his arms holding my elbows, my eyes staring into his.

"You took modern dance?" he asks.

"No." It's hard to concentrate with his face so close to mine. Is the rest of him this perfect? I realise that although he's seen me naked, I've hardly seen any of him. "My focus was on Spanish dancing," I say.

"Spanish dancing, at college?" his face contorts in confusion.

"I learned it from my mother," I say, still lost in his features. "Continuing my training was part of the conditions of my scholarship into drama college. Spanish dancing was what won me the audition."

"You must have been very good," he says, "to win a drama scholarship for dancing."

"Spanish dancing," I correct him. "It's like an act all in itself. A lot of the dance is about the expression on your face."

I haven't thought back to my first audition for years.

He looks impressed. "Then you already have much of the requirement for Tango dancing," he says. "Tango is the dance of love. The best dancers show in their features how the feelings are moving inside them."

I give him a little grin. "Then Spanish dance is the dance of sadness," I say. "So perhaps I am not so adept as you think."

"What do you mean?"

"Real Spanish dancing – from my mother's part of Spain – it is a story of loss. You let your body move through a tale of pain and betrayal."

He gives a half smile, and his voice drops. "I would very much like to see you dance your own way." He has pulled me a little closer.

"Mr Berkeley," I remind him, in a prim voice, "you have brought me here to dance your way. And I am not even sure I will be able to do that."

"Of course." His face breaks into a smile. "How un-gentlemanly of me to forget. Well then, Miss Green, it's time I put you through your paces. What do you understand of Tango?"

"Not very much." I am looking out onto the whirling dancers, feeling unease tighten in my belly. Spanish dance is performed solo. I have less experience of dancing with a partner, although it was a class at school. We learned the waltz – standard acting procedure since this dance is the most common in movies.

"Isabella. I brought you here to show you how pleasurable it can be for a woman to submit to a man."

The words bring a tingling fear to my body.

"In Tango," he says, "the man takes the lead. Do you understand?"

I nod, feeling my mouth dry. I'm not used to dancing with a partner.

"There are certain simple steps which I will teach you," he says. "These steps are always the same, but the direction in which we dance them is determined by me. You dance backwards, always. You must put your total trust in me that I will not lead you into danger."

Into danger? I look out into the dance floor and realise what he means. In the quick steps and movements of the dancers, plotting a course so as not to knock into anyone is tricky.

"It is an exercise in submission," he continues. "You submit your will to me. And in return I pledge to protect you and steer you through a pleasurable dance. Does that sound like something you can do?"

"I… Um. I think so."

"You think so?"

"Yes."

"Then I will show you the steps."

It takes James under ten minutes to decide I have grasped the basic steps, and he seems pleased with my physical memory. "College dance has obviously served you well," he says as he walks me through the eight step dance for the final time.

"Now." He takes me in his arms, straightening me against him in an easy jolt of his powerful arms. "There," he says. "You are standing correctly. At the eighth step, Isabella, there is a pause. At this point I may do what I like with your body, and you must be ready for it."

Do what he likes with my body? I gulp.

"You will feel the slightest touch from my hand at your elbow, steering you the way I wish you to go," he continues. "Do not hesitate to obey me. Any struggle on your part will interfere with my ability to steer you safely across the floor. And the last thing I want to do it lead you into another set of dancers. Understand?" His voice is stern.

I nod. Suddenly the floor ahead of us with its riot of dancers looks incredibly intimidating.

Before I have time to realise what is happening, James sweeps me into the floor. My feet fall into the taught step, and for a moment I concentrate only on counting out the movements.

We complete a set of eight, and James dips me, very slightly, before righting me again and twirling me around back into the floor.

Dancers wheel on either side of us and heading backwards. I have no idea where I'm going. The proximity of other people is within inches, and I know I should be worried I'm about to tunnel into another couple. But held rigidly in James's arms, I feel safe.

Now the steps have arranged themselves in my mind, and instead of counting, I let the music take me. James has a natural affinity for the rhythm of the music, and the exotic sounds crash around us as he meets every step beat perfectly.

I feel myself melding into his strong body, letting it guide me as my feet tap out beneath us. It is easy, effortless.

In Spanish dancing, every sinew of my body is in control, and every thought in mind fixed on the next move and then the next.

This is completely different. I feel as though I haven't a care in the world or a thought in my head besides this powerful man, sweeping me along to the music.

We reach the end of a set of eight, and this time James plunges me almost to the floor. His face is centimetres from mine, and in the final seconds of the pause he sweeps his lips gently against my throat, just brushing the skin.

The effect is an instant erotic surge which charges through my entire body.

He only touched my neck.

As James sweeps me upright and back into the dance, I am struggling to fit what just happened with the formal steps. Then we reach the end of the eight again, and this time James presses me tight against him.

Caught up with the music, I let my foot sweep out, in the same low elegant loop I saw the female dancer complete earlier. My mouth is parted and my eyes half closed as my body arcs into the move, allowing my natural dancer's flexibility to send my leg pirouetting low and wide.

James gathers me up again and the expression on his face is hungry. The thoughts in his head are unmistakable. He pushes me back again, with his exact finesse of power and control, and I realise he is showing me what a relationship with him would be like. He is using the dance to explain to me what he means by obedience. Him in control, deciding the moves, me being swept along, carefree.

What shocks me most about this dynamic is I think I like it.

The thought almost floors me. If it wasn't for James's certain grip on me, propelling me forwards, I feel as though I would stumble. I want this? Do I?

But I realise that I do. Or at least part of me does.

He sweeps me down again, and this time he presses across the line between and around my breasts with his thumb. For a tantalising second, I feel his fingers around my nipple, and the warm arousal floods over my body.

Then he twists me back up again, and I feel my body begging for his touch.

Is this how it would be? I remember his words. *There would be times when you would beg me.* Would he tease me like this? Something tells me he would.

And then another eight step end arrives, and James holds us suddenly still. We stand, close and panting, the longing clear in both of our faces.

The dance has unleashed something in me, and I can't keep my desire for him from showing in my expression.

"I want you," he growls, leaning forward so only I can hear. "I want you to come home with me now. I won't hurt you, Isabella, you have my word. But I want to be inside of you."

I stare up into his handsome features, the dancing and his proximity overwhelming.

"Yes." I say. "Yes James. Take me home."

Chapter 14

James's car is waiting for us as we arrive outside, and he opens the door to allow me inside. I am expecting him to jump on me the moment the doors are closed. But instead he sits upright, looking straight ahead.

I sit next to him wondering once again what is going on in his mind. How can he be so hot one minute and cold the next? A moment ago we were in each other's arms, staring into one another's eyes. Now he could almost be a work colleague sitting next to me.

The car starts up and he leans in close, his mouth brushing my hair. The smell of him is intoxicating.

"Is that a favourite dress?" he asks. I turn to him in confusion.

"No," I reply.

"Good," his voice is low, silky. "Because I am going to rip it off that gorgeous body of yours just as soon as I have you in my bed."

Oh.

I feel my body respond to his words.

"It is taking every ounce of my self-control not to touch you now," he adds. "My hand is itching to slide into that delicious wetness which I know is growing between your legs."

I close my eyes for a minute, hoping it will prevent my blush from being too obvious. How does he know that? I suppose my face must show it all.

Outside, the bright sweep of London Bridge comes into view as the car pulls onto it.

"But I want every part of you ready for what I am about to do to you," he concludes. "So I will not dilute the experience before we reach my apartment."

He turns to face front again, and I am left, red-cheeked beside him. My body, ever the traitor, is already imagining what will happen once we are inside his apartment. My mind is another matter. The turmoil of what it means to be involved with James Berkeley is dimly beginning to register. I am not sure if I can survive it.

The car pulls up into the cobbled street of the apartment, and James comes around to help me out of the car.

After a few curt words to the driver, he performs the complicated code needed to open the sealed door and half drags me over the threshold.

He pulls me against him for a moment, giving me a long kiss which tells of things to come. Then he presses the elevator door and leads me inside.

The doors close noiselessly, and suddenly he has me by the hips, pushed back against the wall. His hands slide up underneath my dress and round to hold my behind. His mouth is on mine, and his hands squeeze. Hard. I let out an involuntary groan and his kiss presses deeper, more urgently. My behind is torn between the pleasure of being held and the slight pain of his tight grip.

The doors open and he releases me. Then, before I know what's happening, he scoops me up into his arms and carries me into his apartment, using his free arm to open the door.

In a few strides we're in his bedroom, and this time, instead of throwing me, he lowers me gently onto the bed.

He stands for a moment, looking at me.

"Isabella," he says. His voice has changed from the lust-charged whisper in the cab to something more like concern.

"Are you sure you want to do this?"

I nod. Lying back there on the bed, arousal coursing through me, there is nothing I want more than for this beautiful man to take me as his own.

"I told you before that you make me gentler," he says, and there is something soft in his voice. "We have already worked on your body, Isabella. It won't be painful for me to be inside you." His voice chokes slightly as he says this, and then he steadies himself. "But I want you to know that emotionally, I care for you."

Wow. This is unexpected.

I nod, not knowing what to say. Do I care for him too?

But before I can analyse my response to his words, his mouth is against mine, taking me in a long kiss, and his fingers are unbuttoning my dress.

"I said I wanted to rip you out of this," he murmurs, as the buttons loosen under his expert fingers. "For now, just seeing you naked will be enough."

I gasp as he pulls the dress over my shoulders, and then his hand snakes around my bra, popping the strap in an easy movement.

His hand floats over my breasts, barely touching the skin. I respond, arching my back into his touch.

Then his fingers travel down.

"Take of your shirt," I gasp, realising he is still fully dressed. He hesitates for a moment and then loosens the first two buttons of his shirt and pulls it free over his head. He unbuttons his trousers, and for the first time, I catch a glimpse of what's to come.

Whoa.

He sees the fear in my face.

"You have nothing to be frightened of, Isabella," he says, his voice hoarse. "My fingers have stretched you sufficiently to accommodate me. And I will be gentle. You have my word."

He tugs off his boxer shorts, freeing his erection, and my doubt turns to genuine terror as I see the size of him.

"I won't hurt you," he promises, catching my expression.

I swallow and nod, trying to believe him.

There is the ripping sound of a foil packet and I realise he has snatched a condom from some hidden place near the bed.

There is a movement I can't see as he rolls it onto himself.

Then his fingers tug apart my thighs, and he is positioned between my legs. I feel him resting there for a moment. His eyes are staring into mine, and his hand moves to caress my cheek.

Then, in a sudden movement, he pushes forward, and he is inside of me.

Oh my God.

The feeling is heavenly and frightening at the same time. The stretch is not painful – not quite – but it feels dangerous.

"Are you ok?" he's still staring into my eyes.

I nod as the warmth washes through me. The pressure inside feels as though he's discovered out new nerve endings which I never knew existed.

He pushes forward again, and this time there is discomfort. Pain, almost.

I wince, and he pulls back slightly. The pain vanishes, leaving only the sweet feeling of pleasure behind.

"Am I hurting you?"

I shake my head.

"Was I hurting you before?"

It feels so strange to speak to him when he is inside me like this.

"A little," I admit, flushing at the feeling of him as I'm talking.

He lifts me a little and props a pillow under the arch of my back. He's still inside me and the change of angle brings another thrill of pleasure.

"We'll try it this way," he says. "Is it painful here?"

"No."

It feels amazing.

"Jeez, Isabella," his eyes are closed suddenly, his expression pained.

"You can't imagine how much I want to thrust hard into you right now."

My face must have showed fear.

"Don't worry," he reassures me. "I promised you I'd be gentle."

He begins to move, slowly, and the feeling of pressure building up is unimaginably good. With every gentle thrust he hits some internal part of me which pulses with pleasure.

I want more, and I groan as he begins to move a little faster inside of me.

He responds with a sudden hard thrust, and I cry out in the pain of it.

James stops and leans close to my face, moving his hand to cover his mouth.

"If you want this," he whispers, "you can't make any noise. Not the slightest sound."

I stay immobile. I don't know if I can promise this. The noise was involuntary. A sheer unchecked cry of pleasure. It came from some person I didn't know existed.

"Hearing you moan with pleasure is the sexiest thing I have ever heard," he says. "If you make another sound I can't be sure that I'll be able to help myself. I might be rough with you. Do you understand?"

At this, I do nod, although I'm still not sure how I'm not to make a sound.

"Shall I keep my hand here, like this?" He asks. I nod again, my eyes wide and timid with his hand covering my mouth. He begins to thrust again, but gentler this time.

As he pushes into me, his movements begin building into an unstoppable rhythm. I can feel deep inside me that his control is expertly judged. Just the slightest bit harder would cause me pain. His tight movements are designed to maximise my pleasure.

Within his measured strokes I feel a sudden urgency build within him. He's close to the edge. The thought thrills me with desire. It brings with it a new urge to cry out, to have him hammer into me.

The thought shocks me and excites me at the same time. With him inside me, his hard body against me, the smell of him, it is impossible to think rationally. I feel every carnal urge rise up and demand to be sated.

I make a small whimper beneath his hand and I feel the sound charge him into a final thrust, pushing deep inside my body. It brings an exquisite mixture of pleasure tinged with pain.

A shock wave of the sensation ricochets through me, and then he sinks his fingers into my hair and explodes into me in a final cry.

He lays on top of me, his hand lost in my hair, his cheek pressed against mine.

Then he raises himself slightly upright, and looks into my eyes. His gaze is confused, wary almost.

"Isabella," he gasps, still panting. "I have never… It has never been this way."

I stare up at him, not knowing what to say, and he catches my mouth in a long kiss.

Then he pulls out of me, rolling off the condom and positioning himself more upright on the bed, so he can look into my face with greater ease.

"I would have liked to make you come," he says.

I feel my cheeks redden, knowing that I didn't have an orgasm. The combination of sensations, the newness of it all. It was all too much.

"Do you think you can come during sex?" he asks gently.

"I… I don't know," I admit. "It's a different feeling, from when you touched me before."

He smiles down at me. "Isabella your body is extremely heightened to an orgasmic response. Have I made you sore?"

The question comes as a surprise, and I mentally assess the area he means.

"No," I say, marvelling at the truth of it.

Between my legs feels like hot and pulsing light. But it doesn't feel painful.

He considers for a moment. Then, very gently, he parts my legs.

His hand brushes my cheek, down to my neck. Then he moves forward, allowing his lips to touch against where his hand is.

The sensation on my skin is so incredibly light. But the feeling it awakens inside of me is anything but. He pulls away from my neck and I stare up at him, wanting him to see the desire in my eyes.

"Then perhaps we should try again," he whispers, "now you are more used to the experience."

Already?

To my amazement, I feel him hard against my thigh again.

"You see the effect you have?" he says, with a slight smile.

This time he pulls my legs forward so they are propped on his hips as he reaches for the condom and rolls it over himself.

He is kneeling between my legs, his knees spread slightly apart. My bottom half is raised towards him, and he holds my thighs in place with a hand under each.

"This is going to be deeper," he warns, "I am going to feel you come, Isabella, whilst I am inside of you."

He reaches his hands lower to come under my buttocks, and grabbing both, heaves me closer. Then with a final pull, he roots himself deep inside me, deeper than anything I've ever felt.

"Oh God, Isabella," he moans, shunting forward even further within me. The sensation brings a jolt of pleasure-pain electricity. "I am looking forward to fucking you hard."

This isn't hard?

The depth of him inside me is terrifying. Although I have to admit it doesn't hurt as I feared it would.

Staring into my eyes, he licks his thumb, and brings it to flick fast over my clitoris.

I arch my back and feel myself squeeze tight around him in the sudden unexpected pulse of sensation.

He moves slowly in and out of me, keeping his thumb at that determined pace, moving so fast the feeling is almost too strong.

"Aaah," I moan, feeling myself tighten in another squeeze. Part of me wants to explode into this feeling and part of it is so intense I am not sure I can handle it.

His thumb slows, and he leans forward to kiss me tenderly on the mouth, tugging gently at my bottom lip with his teeth.

"You didn't think I would let you finish that fast did you?"

His tone is teasing, and I think back to the tango, the relentless back and forth, tease and release.

Is this how it would be with him?

In answer, he thrusts deeply, eliciting from me another involuntary gasp of pleasure. And then he is deeper, harder, but still with a measure of control. He's not giving me his all. Not yet.

Then his thumb returns, slower this time, flicking back and forth over my clitoris in time with his thrusts. He is panting and I can smell his sweat. Every pore in my body wants to drink in every part of him. I want him closer, deeper, to make him part of my very essence.

His thumb starts up the rapid pace again, and I feel myself build to a sudden and rapid height.

James is deep and moving in me. His thumb on my clitoris is exquisite. And then I climax, feeling the deep warmth of him explode through me as a golden sweep of pleasure rushes over my whole body.

I feel myself shudder and pulse, and then, moving more roughly, his hands taking urgent hold of my buttocks as he drives into me.

"I'm going to come," he groans, pushing forward. And then he finishes, sighing out with his eyes tight shut, cupping my buttocks hard in his hand as he orgasms.

From my position beneath him on the bed, I look up at him shyly as he opens his eyes.

"Oh my God, Isabella," he breaths. "The feeling of your tightness, shuddering around me as you came…." He leaves the sentence unfinished, pulling out of me and collapsing next to me in the bed.

I am battling with all the new feelings awakened in me. I have had an orgasm with a man for the first time during sex. Part of me feels relief. Hearing of Lorna's conquests, and my friends at college enjoying sexual exploits, was starting to make me worry what was wrong with me.

Another part of me feels deep joy. I break out into a silly grin, staring into his face.

"I take it that was enjoyable for you?" he smiles.

"Yes," I breathe. "I never imagined it could be like that."

"With you, Isabella, things I have never believed possible have been made true."

I stare at him questioningly for a moment, wondering what he could mean. Perhaps now is not the time to ask. What could James Berkeley not think to be possible? It is a mystery.

I fall asleep in his arms, but wake in the early hours of the morning to find him gone. I come to consciousness slowly, not sure at first where I am. Then it all comes back to me and I sit up in his luxurious bedclothes.

I see a flicker of light under the bedroom door, and wrapping myself in a crisp linen sheet from the bed, I get up to investigate.

Padding quietly into the lounge, the same spectacular view of night-time London is as glorious as ever. And sat on an Eames design-classic chair is James, a laptop on a slim walnut desk in front of him.

He's staring intently at the screen, tapping away, frowning and adjusting his gaze.

"James?"

He looks up and gives me a half smile.

"What are you doing out of bed?"

"Don't you sleep?" I ask.

He smiles again. "Not so much."

"Why not?"

The question seems to catch him off guard.

"I had a period of my life which was… chaotic," he says. "Since that time my sleep has been somewhat erratic. The blessing of it is that I am able to accomplish a great deal more work."

"Is that what you're doing? Work?"

"Yes."

I move across the lounge, hesitantly making my way towards him.

"What are you working on?"

"Take a look."

I thought he may be private about his work, but he gestures I come look at the laptop screen.

I move closer and he draws me onto his lap, so we're both facing the pin-sharp resolution of the images in front of us.

"This is just something I'm playing around with," he says. "I'm experimenting with CGI on pupil dilation."

"What's that?" I stare closer at the screen. Several images are dotted around of a pair of large grey eyes, fringed with thick dark lashes.

"Do you see the pupil in the centre of the eye?" he points to the dark black circle against the grey iris.

"Yes."

"Much expression in the eyes is involuntary. The pupil expands and contracts of its own accord. It gives a lot away."

"What do you mean?"

"Well," he says, tightening his arm a little around my waist. "When a person is frightened or anxious, their pupils get smaller. When they are aroused, or in love, they get larger – they dilate."

"Oh. I didn't know that."

"It's almost impossible to fake," he continues. "Even the best actors can't force their pupils to get smaller or larger. So I'm developing a technology which can change the pupil size artificially, after the scene has been shot. It can make a love or a fight scene more convincing, for example."

"I didn't know that directors did this kind of thing."

"They don't usually," says James. "It's a hobby of mine. When it's developed, I'll sell it to other directors so they can use it."

"Is this something you've done before?"

"Quite a few of the emotional CGI technologies have been developed by me."

He says it without pride or humility.

I look at him in astonishment. Surely that's a major achievement?

"I've got to a new breakthrough," he adds, staring back at the grey eyes on the screen. "I've found an actress whose pupils naturally follow the truth of her acting."

He turns me slightly, so I'm looking into his green eyes. Suddenly I realise what he means.

"Me?" I turn back to the eyes on the screen. "Those are my eyes?"

On his screen they look completely different to the eyes I see in the mirror. It must be the flattery of the camera, I decide.

"Yes," he turns back to look at his screen. "I owe you a debt of gratitude, Isabella. Your natural ability has helped me detail several emotional responses which had eluded me."

Oh.

I look back at the screen, uncertain what to say. The grey eyes stare back at me, frightened, happy, angry, sad.

The bewildering range of expressions reflect how I feel inside, I realise, when I'm with Berkeley. His proximity is still like a drug to me. But my head is in turmoil.

"Go back to bed, Isabella," says James. And without registering that he's ordering me like a child, I obey.

Chapter 15

The next morning, I wake to see James smiling down at me.

"You look so peaceful when you're asleep," he says. "Are you hungry?"

I nod sleepily.

"I'll fix you some breakfast," he says. "Do you like coffee? Tea?"

"Coffee. Thanks." I stare after him appreciatively as he exits the bedroom. A man who wakes you up with coffee and a promise of breakfast. I could get used to this.

Suddenly I remember Lorna. I didn't tell her I'd be out all night. She's probably worried about me. I slip out of bed and find my underwear, cast about from the previous night. The memory of it gives me an unexpected flush of pleasure.

I dress quickly, throwing on my vintage dress but not my jeans, and walk barefoot into the giant lounge.

James is in the kitchen area with his back to me, and I see my phone on top of one of his uber-chic speakers. I pick it up and flip it over to see a screen full of messages and calls from Lorna.

I sigh, and send her a quick message.

Stayed with James. Don't worry. Back soon.

She'll be mad I haven't called her to fill her in with the juicy details, but this will have to do for the time being. Predictably the screen buzzes with a flashing incoming call. Lorna. I flick it to silent feeling guilty. I'll make it up to her later on today.

I walk over to the kitchen area and see that James is looking at a newspaper spread out on the worktop.

"Anything happen I should know about?" I say.

He is silent for a moment and then he replies.

"I think so, yes." His voice is strained.

My gaze falls on the front page of the newspaper and I realise why. I gasp in shock.

"That's us!"

Plastered over the front page of the newspaper is a close-up shot of James and me. We're at the *Cathedral de Tango*, and James has me bent backwards in a classic dance pose. Our faces are almost touching, and even from the newspaper page, the chemistry between us is electric.

"I thought the Cathedral was paparazzi free," says James. He's obviously not pleased, and my heart does a cold flip of disappointment. He's ashamed to be seen publicly with me.

He flips open the newspaper and the next page is a double-page spread of us tango dancing. The headline reads: "James Berkeley with Mysterious Dancer."

Mysterious dancer. That's me. It would be funny if it wasn't for the fact he seems so angry.

His fist slams the page suddenly, and I flinch in shock.

"I thought I had taken all the necessary precautions," he mutters, staring at the pictures.

I let my eyes fall on the photographs. In them I look like someone else. It's hard to match the quiet Issy I know with the tango dancer in the pictures. Her face is a perfect picture of passion, her body perfectly moulded to Berkeley's.

We look made for each other. I wonder what that says about us. Was he acting a part? Is this what lust looks like?

He flips another page, and there, in black and white, is a picture of Madison Ellis.

The familiar face has a sudden new resonance now that I know her as Berkeley's wife. She wears sunglasses, and her famous features look tired.

My stomach turns to ice. *His wife. How could I have forgotten?*

In the passion and excitement of James Berkeley, the fact he was married had completely slipped my mind.

A marriage of convenience. I tell myself. *Or at least that's what he told you*. The sudden possibility rises as a sickening possibility.

I almost gasp out loud, wondering if I've been caught in the classic married man scenario. It would certainly explain why the pictures have made him so mad. As I consider things, this notion becomes more and more certain.

Why else would he be so upset to see our picture in the papers?

On the kitchen countertop, Berkeley's phone rings. The buzz against the wood surface makes us both jump.

James snatches it up. But not before I see the name on the display.

Maddy.

Maddy. Not Madison. Or Madison Ellis. What kind of name is that for a marriage of convenience?

I feel as though I'm going to throw up. What if he's been lying to me all along and stupid naïve girl that I am, I didn't know any better? Perhaps James Berkeley really is cheating on his wife and I'm just the other woman.

The possibility brings with it an unexpected numbness.

"Hello, Maddy." James swings away from me to take the call.

In that one movement, it's as though someone has poured cold water all over me. I stand for a moment, almost gasping in the sudden chill of realisation.

He's angry to be seen with you in the paper. He's taking his wife's call. He calls her Maddy.

I make for the bedroom.

Once inside my eyes sweep the designer furnishings, looking for my remaining clothes.

I grab them up, not bothering to put my jeans on. My eyes rest on his gift of the Jimmy Choo shoes which I had slid my feet into so happily only last night.

Now the tears come. I shake my head. The shoes can stay. I would rather die than wear something he bought me.

I remember the Chanel suit back at my apartment. I'll get rid of that later. For now, I have to get home.

I race out of the bedroom, tears streaming down my face, still barefoot and clutching my jeans and purse.

My phone. I grab it.

James still has his back to me, talking on the phone.

"The earliest you could arrive would be 5pm," he's saying. "You could take my private jet."

This final sentence destroys any hope I had left. He's inviting her to London, eager to make amends. I can't hear anymore. I run for the door and make my way fast down the staircase. The metal is cold on my bare feet, but I can hardly feel it.

All I feel is a sick hot feeling of betrayal in my heart.

Then I'm out in the cold morning air of London, and the cobbles are like ice under my feet.

A black cab trundles by, and I hail it with relief, hoping I've enough money in my purse to get back to Chelsea.

The driver slows, and I pull open the door and climb into the back.

"Are you alright love?" the driver's eyes are warm and concerned.

I nod yes. "Chelsea please," I manage in a choked voice.

"Right you are."

He swings away, just as I hear someone calling my name.

James Berkeley is out on the street, also barefoot, and shouting after me.

"Someone for you?" asks the cabbie, slowing very slightly.

"Just drive." I blink, letting the tears fall, and the cab pulls away fast.

I hear my name shouted down the street again, but I don't look around.

As we pull over London Bridge, I allow myself a few deep sobs, before trying to pull myself together. I'll have time to cry later. Right now I have to make sure I have money to pay for the cab.

I fumble through my things, grab out my phone, and call Lorna. She picks up immediately.

"Oh my God!" she shrieks down the phone. "How was he? What was it like?"

"Lorna," I say, "I'm in a cab."

Her whole tone changes instantly when she hears the anguish in my voice. I really must sound terrible.

"Oh my God, Issy. What's wrong? What's wrong, Issy? Are you ok?"

"I'm fine," I lie, trying to keep my voice steady.

"What did he do?"

"Nothing… It's just. I'm in a cab and I don't know if I'll have enough money. I've only got a twenty pound note."

"Ok, honey." Lorna is all business. "Don't you worry about that. I've got loads of cash. I'm coming down now. I'll be waiting on the doorstep."

I close my eyes tight, thanking the world I have such a good friend.

"We'll talk about it then, ok?"

"Ok." I can barely get the word out.

"Don't you worry Issy," says Lorna. "We'll get some ice-cream, and some movies and have a girl day, just the two of us. You can tell me all about it. You'll be feeling fine soon."

"Yeah," I whisper, knowing my world has just ended. "I'll be fine."

Chapter 16

Lorna is waiting for me as promised, with a handful of notes.

"I would have taken her all the way home, even without the full fair," says the cabbie to Lorna as she helps me out. "She's obviously been through a lot, poor girl."

This sudden sympathy brings another juddering grip of silent tears, and I nod in thanks at the driver.

Lorna pushes a bunch of notes into his hands as he stares after me in concern.

"Is she going to be alright?" he asks Lorna, reaching to pass her some change.

Lorna nods, dismissing the change, and putting her arm around my shoulder.

"Keep the tip. I'll look after her. Thanks for bringing her home."

Lorna leads me inside, and I lean gratefully on her shoulder as we ride the elevator up to the apartment.

Once inside, I slump onto the sofa, bury my head in my hands and sob.

Lorna keeps a tactful distance for a few minutes, making me a hot drink in the kitchen. Then she returns with two steaming cups of cocoa and moves in next to me on the couch, tucking her long legs underneath her.

"Do you want to talk about it, honey?" she asks, brushing a piece of dark hair out of me face.

"I'm an idiot," I say, "a complete and utter idiot." The confession brings with it a fresh bout of sobbing. Lorna's face shows concern.

"He told me it was a marriage of convenience," I say, managing to find a little of my voice through the tears. "Then we got papped, last night, at a tango club."

Lorna raises her eyes at the mention of a tango club but says nothing.

"When he saw the pictures in the paper, he was furious," I say, the memory bringing another flurry of tears. "Then he took a call from his wife. I think he was arranging for her to fly over from LA."

Lorna nods, thinking about this.

"Honey, are you sure you're not over-reacting," she says gently. I look at her through bleary eyes.

"What do you mean?"

"Well. Just because he's angry about the pictures, it doesn't mean that his marriage isn't a sham like he told you."

"What else would it mean?"

Lorna shrugs. "I don't know. A lot of famous people hate being papped. James Berkeley strikes me as the kind of man who would want to protect his personal life."

"Then why take a call from his wife?" I am adamant. "He's been lying to me, Lorna."

I visualise the pictures of Madison Ellis in the papers. Even in her forties, she's a classic screen beauty, with big blue wide-apart eyes and a sweep of sexy blonde hair.

What was I thinking? Why on earth would James Berkeley choose me over her?

"Ok, honey," says Lorna, obviously deciding not to push the issue. "Whatever you want. How about we stay in and watch some movies?"

I nod, feeling pathetic and sorry for myself.

"Here, I'll put your things away." Lorna gestures for the pile of crumpled clothing still clutched in my arms.

I remember the Chanel suit.

"Throw the suit out," I say. "The one he bought me."

Lorna's eyes widen. "The Chanel suit? Issy, that's a lovely suit. It was a gift. Are you sure you don't want to keep it?"

I shake my head. "Throw it out."

"I'll find someone to give it to," decides Lorna. "I've got plenty of model friends who it would fit."

I nod to her. She turns to leave and my phone tumbles from the pile of clothing in her arms.

"Here," she picks it up from the floor and hands it to me.

I take it, and see twenty missed calls and ten messages on the screen. I've had it on silent, I realise, since I flicked it on for Lorna's earlier call.

It seems like a lifetime ago that I clicked that switch. Only a few seconds later and my world fell apart. Funny how things go.

The calls are all from Berkeley, and the messages are too. They don't say much, only petition me to get in touch.

The last reads:

Why won't you talk to me?

In a fit of sudden anger, I punch in a text back.

You have your wife to talk to.

Then I delete his messages and toss the phone onto the couch. It begins ringing again. Him. I silence it and toss it down.

There's a buzz at the door, and I have a sickening feeling of who it might be.

Lorna appears in the doorway, her face anxious.

"Do you think that's him?"

I nod.

"Do you want to see him?" She looks like she wants me to.

I shake my head stubbornly. I refuse to be the other woman. And a part of me knows I would find it hard to resist him in person.

"Please, Lorna. Will you get rid of him for me? I don't want to see him."

Lorna hesitates for a moment and then walks away.

There's a click as she exits the apartment. A few moments later, she's back, looking upset.

"Well I sent him away, but are you sure you won't speak to him, Issy? He looks dreadful."

Good.

I shake my head again.

"Ok. Well." Lorna takes a breath. "Ready for the movieathon? I've got no castings today. We'll just sit and eat and watch TV."

I give her a weak smile. Beside me on the couch, I see my phone flash into life again. *James Berkeley*, reads the display. I pick it up and turn it off with a determined click.

"That sounds good."

It's four movies and a whole tub of ice-cream later when the door buzzes again. Berkeley has stopped calling, and my emotions have been lulled into a state of numb calm by sugar and Patrick Swayze.

The sound makes us both start.

"Him again?" asks Lorna.

I shrug. "I don't think so."

"If it is, I'll send him away."

Lorna stands and exits the room to pick up the entry buzzer phone.

I don't hear the other half of the conversation, but I hear her say: "I'll buzz you up."

I sit a little upright on the couch, wondering who it is. I look awful and don't relish the idea of explaining my red eyes and couch-potato chic to one of Lorna's model friends.

"Who is it?" I ask as Lorna walks wide-eyed back into the room.

"You won't believe this," she says. "It's Madison Ellis. She's asking for you."

Chapter 17

Madison Ellis makes a shy little knock on our apartment door, and Lorna opens it.

"She's in here," Lorna says.

Madison appears in the doorway, her iconic features full of concern. She's tiny in every way, and beside her Lorna's model height looks towering.

Her famous features look prettier in real life, and less intimidating. She wears a simple shift dress with knee high boots, and her blonde hair is fanned angelically around her face.

"May I come in?" she says. Her voice comes out almost as a whisper, but I recognise the tone from the movies.

"Yes," I say, uncertain of what to make of all this. Madison Ellis is in my apartment.

She walks forward and then positions herself uncertainly on the couch. Lorna mouths "are you ok?" and then retreats when I nod.

"Cookie-dough," says Madison, looking at the ice-cream tub. "That's my favourite when I'm sad too."

Madison Ellis eats ice-cream? She's a size zero.

"Of course, I have to go on a six mile jog afterwards," she says, with a little smile. "I'm not a lovely young woman like you anymore."

Great. She's also nice, I think sulkily.

"James says you won't return his calls," she says.

I sit up a little.

"And he also says he thinks it's because of me," she adds.

I have a sudden and horrible feeling that I've got things completely and utterly wrong.

"I wanted you to know that there has never been anything between James and I," she says, fixing me with a steady gaze from her big blue eyes. "It's a Hollywood marriage. For the cameras. I owe James my career," she adds.

She's looking at me intently, as though she's genuinely concerned.

"I…" I'm trying to speak, but no words are coming out. I simply cannot believe that this beautiful woman has come to my home to try and fix up things between me and Berkeley. And how wrong I've been to doubt him.

The realisation brings with it a crimson blush, which lights up my entire face.

"You didn't have to come all this way," I manage.

She smiles, a big warm smile. "I was flying to England in any case."

"You flew to England today? And then you came to see me?"

This is getting worse and worse. I can't believe she has come to my house after a nine hour flight.

"I am so, so sorry." I sigh, and rub my forehead. "I… I can't believe you've come over here. I'm so sorry. You must be tired."

She smiles again and waves dismissively. "James's happiness means a lot to me," she says. "He might seem like an ogre to some, but he genuinely cares for people." She's looking at me intently again. "And I think he's had some issues in his past which haven't been resolved."

Now I'm interested.

"What issues?"

"James never talks about his past," says Madison. "At least not to my knowledge." She looks at me acutely for a moment, as if wondering if he's said anything to me.

"Oh."

"He's in pieces. Really," she adds. "He's desperate to speak to you. And I think he knows he messed up."

Did he? Suddenly I'm not so sure. In fact, I'm pretty convinced it's me who messed things up.

"I think I overreacted," I admit, realising the truth of the words as I say them. Something about Madison encourages confidence. I wonder if this is how she rose to stardom. "I lost my temper."

My famous temper, I think wryly. My mother always said my Spanish hot-headedness would get me into trouble.

Madison laughs at this last confession, and leans over to pat my knee.

"Then you and James will make a great couple," she says.

"Look, Madison," I still can't believe I'm talking to her.

"Maddy," she says.

"Um. Maddy." *This is unreal.* "I'm really sorry you had to come over. Truly."

"That's alright." She reaches over and gives my cheek a soft little pinch. It's the kind of gesture which would seem much too forward from anyone else. But coming from her, it seems like the most natural thing in the world. I feel like I've known her forever.

"I have a feeling I'll be seeing a lot more of you," she says. "I've never seen James this smitten before. And don't worry. I'll tell him to take care of you. Such a beautiful girl."

Take care of me. If only she knew.

She stands, smiling. "I'll see myself out," she says. "Perhaps when I'm less jet-lagged, you can come over to my place sometime and we'll eat some cookie-dough ice-cream."

"Uh. Yeah. Sure."

"I'll see myself out." And with a last charming smile, she's gone.

I sit back on the couch, star struck and reeling from all of this. Part of me is a little annoyed with James. What sort of man sends a Hollywood A-lister to petition for a girl to take his phone calls?

But the thought takes my heart in a happy warm hold, and I grin to myself. Ok I've been stupid and I've over-reacted. Yes I'm embarrassed - mortally embarrassed - that a famous actress has just seen me red-eyed on the couch. But despite all of this, I don't care.

James likes me. Madison said so. And he hadn't lied to me. His marriage isn't real. I hug the thought to myself, grinning.

Lorna appears in the doorway, her face a picture.

"So, all good in tinsel-love-town?" she says, a huge smile on her face. "Did a certain person get the wrong end of the stick?"

I laugh. "Yes. Yes. Ok, you were right. I was wrong. There is nothing between him and his wife. It's just for show."

Lorna collapses next to me on the couch.

"Phew! Issy Green. Your life! You could be a movie all of your own. I knew you were a good actress, but I didn't think I'd be welcoming in Hollywood royalty *quite* so soon!"

I laugh again, and Lorna joins me.

"It's crazy, huh?" I admit, still trying to assess things myself.

"Yeah," says Lorna. "All these years you've been holding out on us. Then, wham! You have enough love life drama for three people."

She looks at me intently.

"So, I take it lover boy is off the hook?"

"Yeah. I guess so."

"Then you best go call him, Miss Leading Lady."

I raise myself to my feet, my face still plastered with an idiot grin, and take my phone.

"Just going to make a call in my bedroom," I say.

"Of course you are." Lorna picks up the remote and flicks the channel. "I'm going to try and find something more interesting than your life to watch on TV, but I think I'm out of luck."

I leave the room, heading for my bedroom, and collapse on the bed, clicking on my phone.

It takes five minutes to inform me of all the missed calls, voicemails and messages. Then finally my phone is functional and I press the contact. James Berkeley. I take a deep breath as it rings.

For a terrible second, I think he's not going to pick up. Then his voice is loud and relieved over the phone.

"Isabella."

"James."

I wonder if he can hear the embarrassment in my voice. "You didn't have to send Madison over," I mumble, part shame, part amusement.

"When you have an important person to win over, you pull out all the stops," he says. "That's my attitude to business. It's not different in my personal life."

"And I'm an important person?" I tease, delighted to have drawn this confession out of him.

He sighs down the phone, and I can almost hear his eyes close.

"You have no idea how important," he says. "Can I come up?"

"Come up?"

"I'm outside," he says.

"You're outside?"

"If you're going to keep repeating everything I say then this relationship is never going to work."

Relationship? He wants a relationship?

I stop myself from repeating him again.

"Why are you outside?" I manage.

"I've been here all day," he says. "I was hoping, since you're not answering your phone, you might venture out. But I was disappointed."

"Sure," I manage, not sure what to make of that. "Come up."

He's at my door in moments, and this time I answer it instead of Lorna. She sits grinning from the couch, rolling her eyes at my sudden dramatic romantic life.

"Hi," I say shyly, as I open the door.

"Hi." He takes my chin in his hands and stares into my eyes.

I am conscious that Lorna is only a few metres away in the next room, and take his hand.

"Come through." I lead him to my bedroom.

"The second time I've been in here," he murmurs, seating himself on my bed and drawing me down next to him. "And yet it feels like we've known each other so long."

The truth of it surprises me. I realise we've been dating each other – if you could call it that - only a matter of days.

His proximity comes with the familiar allure. I can smell him, feel his warmth.

James leans towards me, catching me in his arms.

We kiss and I feel the world melt away. My body is writhing with the familiar electric current which he manages to spark in me. Our lips are hot, fervent, and his hands slide around my waist, pulling me closer.

"God, Issy," he says, "what have you done to me?"

"I could ask you the same," I breathe.

In answer, he slides his hands up my body, caressing my breasts and pressing his thumbs gently into my nipples.

I push forward into his hands, eager for his touch.

Then he reaches a hand up under my skirt and tugs down my panties.

It feels too sudden, too intimate, but at the same time incredibly hot. I haven't the force of will to stop him. I don't want to.

He roughly pulls away my underwear, leaving my lower half naked beneath my dress.

Then he's pushing me back, and he's rested on top of me.

"I. Want. You. So Badly." He's kissing me hard between each word, and then I hear a foil packet tear as he frees his erection from his jeans and rolls a condom onto himself.

I tear at his shirt, ripping it open and exposing the taut muscles of his chest.

He waits for a moment, poised between my legs, and it's agonising. Every part of me is screaming for him. Then he plunges in, taking my mouth in a deep kiss as he thrusts inside.

This time, it's hard, fast. But I want it. I want him to take me roughly.

I moan as he moves, pushing strongly against me, his hardness penetrating deep and then deeper. I claw at the strong muscles of his arms as they circle around and under me.

This time, the feelings of fear and pain have gone. There's nothing but the smell of him, his mouth on mine, and him, taking me completely.

I feel myself letting go, opening myself up to his strength.

Then I feel the orgasm begin to build. He moves harder, and then repositions himself so he's hitting a new place on intense pleasure deep within.

It's so intense, this sudden physical reunion after a day of trying to push him from my mind. The feelings of relief mingle with my desire for him.

I moan again, and he thrusts hard. It's too much, and I gasp as the feeling grows to the inescapable climax of pleasure.

I cry out, shattering into the warmth of my orgasm. He groans and makes two more deep hard thrusts. The sensation raises me into another exquisite spasm and he groans as he comes inside of me.

He lies on top of me, both of us still half-dressed, taking in the sudden pulse of lust which brought us together. James pulls out of me, rolling to one side, and wraps his arms around me.

He pushes his mouth against my ear.

"I take it you've forgiven me," he says.

I laugh. "For the time being," I say.

He sits up, looking troubled for a moment, drawing me upright with him.

"I owe you an apology," he says. His face looks chastised. Sad.

I look at his features in puzzlement, trying to work out what he needs to be sorry for.

"I was so angry when I saw those pictures in the newspaper," he says. "I… I failed to protect you, Issy. I know this industry. You don't. It's my duty to protect you from those vultures. I thought I'd done that, but I hadn't. I let your picture make it to press. It's unforgivable."

He looks so sad, and I put my arm around him. His words have taken me completely by surprise. He was worried about protecting me?

"What are you protecting me from?" I say, trying to understand.

He turns to me. "The paparazzi, of course. There's no way I'm going to let you become fodder for their newspapers."

"I... I don't mind if a few pictures appear," I say. From what I remember, they were nice pictures.

James is shaking his head.

"You are new to this," he repeats, "and trust me, Issy, if you let me direct you in this movie, you'll be a big star. Soon. But you have to keep out of the press. They only want to run bad news."

Ok, so all the news stories I read on celebrities in the English press tend to be about scandal. I think about this.

"I've got my best lawyers on this," he says. "I've got every one of those paps scared for their jobs. You're protected, for a time at least."

"Are you ashamed of me?" I ask. I can't help myself.

He smiles. "Of course I'm not. But my life is complicated. Madison and I have an arrangement. Believe me, if I hadn't taken strong action today, tomorrow's papers would be running stories of you as a marriage wrecker. That's why Madison has flown in. We've worked out a story to limit the damage and keep you safe."

My mind is wheeling.

"What story?" I manage.

"That you're a dance teacher, and I'm learning to tango for a vow renewal which Madison and I are planning."

Oh. This hurts me more deeply than I would have thought.

He sees my expression.

"It's for the best, Issy," he murmurs. "Nothing is more important than keeping you safe. My lawyers have informed all the papers that any more pursuit of the dance teacher will be dealt with under the utmost power of my legal team."

"So I'm just a dance teacher," I mumble. All my earlier feelings are starting to return. I'm nothing to him. His image is more important.

"Oh, Issy," he says. "You're so much more than that."

"Then what am I?" I demand, suddenly angry again.

He gives me an impish grin.

"You're the girl who ran barefoot out of my house rather than wear a pair of shoes I bought you. You certainly have a lot of spirit."

I flush at the memory.

"Did you think that I'd lied to you?" he asks gently. "About Madison?"

This is too embarrassing. I did, but now that the facts are in front of me, I have to admit I had no reason to think it.

"Yes," I admit, looking down.

"I'm sorry I took her call when I should have been explaining things to you," he says. "But I was so frantic to protect you. It had to be done quickly."

He's staring intently into my face.

"I admire your spirit, Issy, but this tendency to over-react might need to be managed."

I stare back at him, not knowing what he means. He sighs.

"Have you thought about my suggestion, Issy?" he says. "Wouldn't you like me to take that tempestuous nature in hand? It would be so much easier for both of us."

"I… I don't know." It is true that my temper has gotten me into scrapes in the past. But that doesn't mean I want to be led by a man.

"Think about it," he says. "I think that being ruled by me would do you more good than you know. That and a well-timed beating now and again."

I take a breath.

He gives a roguish smile.

Is he serious? I can't tell.

"Are you really saying that you want to beat me?" I ask, swallowing at the thought.

"I want you to submit to my authority," he says. "And when you over-react as you did today, a punishment would be needed to keep you in line."

"What sort of punishment?" I am curious despite myself.

His eyes flash. "Something pre-agreed by both of us."

James lowers his voice and takes my chin in his hand.

"I think that a part of you wants very badly to be taken in hand," he says, fixing me with a steely gaze. "Your rebellious nature wants to be subdued."

He releases my chin, and I feel strangely disappointed.

"Only time will tell," he says. "And as you know, Isabella, I would never do anything you hadn't agreed to."

"So what will you do now?" I ask, changing the subject.

He seems amused.

"What do you mean?"

"You and Madison. I suppose you have some public engagements. So you can reassure the world you're happily married?" The last words come out bitterly. I can't help myself.

"Yes," he says. "We have a premier tonight which we will both attend. Our PRs have already explained the tango situation to the press."

The tango situation. My eyes fill with tears.

"Issy," he says gently. All the fire has left his face, and he sweeps my wet cheek with his thumb. "You have no idea what you mean to me. Today, when I thought I might have lost you..." he lets the words hang.

"I've spoken to Madison," he continues. "We've agreed that the marriage has done all it can to help her career. She's back in the A-list now. She's happy. As soon as it's appropriate, we'll begin making it obvious we're leading separate lives. It won't happen overnight. But it is happening."

He's leaving Madison?

"Is Madison happy with that?" I ask. I am in shock.

"Madison and I are very good friends," he says carefully. "She wants me to be happy and she knows this is what I want."

"Are you doing this for me?" The thought is too preposterous.

"Who else would I be doing it for?"

I frown, confused.

"It's all so much," I admit. "Everything has happened so quickly. Part of me has strong feelings for you. Part of me is unsure."

Like the fact that you want to subdue me.

He nods, looking sad.

"I couldn't ever expect that a girl like you would consider me," he says. "I'm not a walk in the park, Issy. But I want to make the situation right, so you can at least decide with everything clear."

"And that includes divorcing your wife?" as I say the words they sound ridiculous.

"Stage wife," he says. "Not my real wife. Our relationship has come to a natural end. This way you can decide for yourself. But I warn you," he voice turns dark, "you may still decide you can't have a relationship with me. I'm not even sure I'd want you too."

"This is the obedience thing," I say slowly.

"Yes."

I nod, assessing this.

"I'm not an old-fashioned girl," I say, thinking of my upbringing. "My parents ran puppet-shows. It was all very bohemian."

He laughs at this admission.

"It sounds charming. When am I going to meet your mother?"

"My mother?"

"You told me your father had passed away. Otherwise, naturally I would want to be introduced to him as well."

"Yes. Um. Well. My mother. She lives out in the countryside."

I remember suddenly that my mother is planning to come to London soon. Though I can't recall which day we arranged. I'll have to check my diary. I try to picture my mother meeting Berkeley, but the image doesn't come.

"She's coming to London soon, but I think it might be too soon for you to meet her," I explain.

"I see." His eyes are questioning me.

"She's a little unusual," I manage.

"With a daughter like you, I wouldn't expect anything else."

"Well perhaps I can meet her when you decide you're ready," he concludes.

"What about your parents?" I say, to change the subject.

"What about them?"

"What are they like?"

"There's only one remaining," he says. "My mother died when I was a very young boy, in Mauritius."

I piece this together with what I know of him. So he was brought up with his mother in Mauritius and then packed off the boarding school in England.

"Did you get sent to boarding school when she died?" I ask tentatively.

"Yes." He is terse, making it clear no more questions are to be asked.

"What about your father?" I ask, steering the conversation over to something else.

James gives a cold laugh. "My father. Well. There's a story." He pauses for a moment. "I guess you'll get the chance to find out. Would you like to meet him?"

Would I? I'm not sure.

"When?"

"In a few weeks," he says. "I've made arrangements to visit the estate. You could come with me."

The estate?

"Where exactly does your father live?" I ask, hedging for an answer.

He laughs again, obviously aware that I'm delaying my answer.

"In the countryside," he says. "I think you'll like it."

His phone beeps and he frowns.

"Think about it," he says, "we'd only be there one night." He stands, and leans down to kiss my forehead.

"I have to go and play the dutiful husband," he says. And my heart twists in my chest.

Chapter 18

Whilst James plays the husband figure, Lorna has dragged me out for yet another party night. She's sure it will take my mind off the situation, and maybe she's right. Though I hate to admit it, the thought of James leading Madison up the red carpet makes me feel sick with jealously.

Lorna's pulled some strings to arrange an evening with two of her modelling friends at the Met Bar, and all three of them are getting into the swing of things.

I'm wearing an orange and black retro-print dress, which is the best I could do from my wardrobe to keep up with the models. On the London streets, I could usually be considered fashionable. My wardrobe is full of vintage buys and clever second-hand finds, and I can always pull an interesting outfit together. But alongside Lorna and her model friends, and their access to the latest designer releases, I don't have a hope.

"Tell me again why we're drinking here?" I say, taking in the designer lighting concept which casts the sixties-style tables into things of glamorous beauty.

"The agency has an arrangement with the bar," says Alex, looking at me with mock-seriousness over his horn-rimmed glasses. "We supply the eye candy, they supply the drinks."

"Which means we get to drink at the Met Bar," says Lorna, "while all the other people our age are searching out the pint-pitcher deals in Trafalgar Square."

We're sitting on a black vinyl table with a jug of pre-mixed cocktail. Sandy, a blonde Claudia Schiffer lookalike from Houston, wrinkles her nose as she sips her drink.

"Sweet," she says, swallowing the sticky liquid and tugging her low-cut white dress down a little further.

Sandy schooled at Yale and managed to ditch her Southern accent along the way. But that doesn't stop most English people from thinking she's a dumb model. It used to drive her crazy, but she's learned to play up to it.

"That's what you get when the drinks are free," says Alex, a skinny male-model with oversized retro glasses and artistic tattoos covering his arms.

"God bless Select Modelling agency for supplying us with low-quality drinks in such an upmarket establishment." Alex is technically an artist, but his quirky looks got him spotted last year, and now he fronts major designer campaigns.

"Bottoms up!" says Lorna, raising her mineral water in a mock toast. She's sensibly sticking to sugar-free soft drinks tonight, filling me with relief. It's one of my real fears that Lorna will get carried away drinking and have a diabetic episode.

I chink my own glass – a mix of water with a splash of cocktail in it. Since Berkeley, I have found myself brave enough to drink alcohol again, but I'm not about to get drunk.

The Met Bar is attached to one of London's most glamorous hotels and has a notoriously difficult entry policy. I was amazed to get in, until Lorna talked me through the deal with her agency.

"I think the choice of bar might also have something to do with a certain gentleman," adds Sandy, raising her glass and eyebrows at Lorna.

For once, Lorna looks a little embarrassed.

"He only said he might be here," she says, fiddling with her napkin.

"Wait," I say, "are you talking about Ben Gracey?"

I had forgotten about him entirely. In the last few days, I've thought of nothing but Berkeley, and my selfishness hits me full force in the face. I haven't asked anything about Lorna's love life.

"Lorna, I'm so sorry. Did you two hook up?"

She turns to me, bashful.

"Yeah, well. No. Not exactly. He *is* cute," she says shyly. "And he texted to say he might show up tonight."

I can't believe it. Lorna. Shy. Waiting for a man. A man who says he *might* show up. This is not like her at all. I think back to what I remember of Ben but not much comes to mind. Then again, I did have him contrasted with the force of nature that is James Berkeley. Hardly a fair comparison.

"Well he's a lucky guy," I manage, wondering what he's pulled to have this effect on her.

"Here's to lucky guys," opines Alex, raising his glass for yet another toast. Alex is gay, and with his model good looks, could actually be considered one of the luckiest men on the male scene. At least, if you define luck by quantity.

"Here, here," says Sandy, taking another sip. She smacks her lips at the sweet drink. "I might stick to the water," she says.

"No way," says Alex, leaning over to top up her glass. "We are finishing this jug. It's free."

"Ok," acknowledges Sandy. "But then we head up to the rock clubs in Camden and party with people our own age."

I look around the Met Bar and realise she's right. I've spotted a fair few celebrities in here and even more obviously wealthy people. But the average age is over forty. No wonder Lorna's modelling agency has a deal with the bar. We're the youngest people here.

I excuse myself to visit the bathroom and head to the shining tiled luxury of the Met Bar toilets.

"Someone's in a hurry."

I've bumped full force into a linen shirt and designer suit jacket, and straighten up to apologise.

"Hey, Isabella."

"Oh," I recognise the face suddenly. It's Ben Gracey. "Hey Ben."

"Listen, I'm on my way to see Lorna at that table," he says. "But I just wanted to apologise for my behaviour the other night."

The other night? I remember the unlicensed cab, Berkeley's anger.

"Oh. Right," I say. "Don't worry about it."

"No, truly." He stops me with a gentle hand. "I'm really sorry. I'd had a few too many drinks and was all swept up with you gorgeous girls." He gives a charming smile, and I feel myself warm to him.

Only someone with that aristocratic English accent could say that last line without sounding cheesy. He's from the same class as James Berkeley, I realise. And then I remember that they're relatives.

"I hear you're seeing more of James Berkeley," adds Ben.

I pause, wondering how to respond. Can I admit it publicly?

"Lorna told you?" I guess, silently promising to kill her when I get back to the table.

"Yes. Don't be angry. She had your best interests at heart. She doesn't trust him, Isabella."

She doesn't? That's news to me.

"At least, not recently," he corrects himself.

"What do you mean?"

Ben lowers his voice and leans in urgently.

"Listen, Isabella. I grew up with James Berkeley. I know more about him than most. You need to be careful."

You don't know the half of it, I think wryly.

"He got into trouble at school," he continues.

"Yes," I say, finding myself rising to James's defence. "He was expelled. He told me."

"Oh." Ben looks confused. Angry almost.

"And I expect he didn't tell you why he wasn't welcome in his father's house for a time."

"No," I say, coldness settling around me. "He didn't."

Ben's voice is low, urgent.

"Berkeley had a problem with drugs," he says, showing me with his eyes that he means a serious problem. "You need to be careful, Isabella. He's unstable. Not good news at all."

"I…" I stare at Ben, not knowing what to say. This sudden new information has hit me hard. Can I stand any more rollercoaster emotions today about James Berkeley?

"Well, thanks," I manage. "I'll bear that in mind." And I head towards the bathroom trying to compute this information.

I enter the sweep of glittering mirrors and expensive toiletries and stare at my reflection.

"What are you doing, Isabella Green?" I mutter to myself. "What are you doing with this man?"

I look at myself for a long time, trying for an answer, but nothing comes.

James has told me himself that he's dangerous. Unsuitable. That he has a strange requirement that I acquiesce to his will. Then I remember what Ben told me about the contracts which James made his actresses sign.

But that wasn't true? Was it?

I try to piece together what I know. James denied it. I believed him. Could Ben be making all of this up? Obviously, they're not friends. I could see that by their terse exchange in the car the previous night. But some instinct tells me Ben is right about the drug problem. I remember James's face when he talked about his ex-girlfriend and a rush of jealousy courses through me.

A drug overdose. Those were his words. *She died of a drug overdose.*

All I can do is ask him. But for all the unfair mistrust I've shown, I'm not sure he deserves to be interrogated.

Then I realise there is another way to find out. There is at least one advantage to dating a famous man.

Pulling out my phone, I open an internet search page.

I hesitate for a moment, and then, before I can change my mind, I Google: *'James Berkeley, drugs'*.

The moment I press 'search' I regret the decision. It seems unfair that because James is famous I can delve into his private history, but he can't look at mine.

Nevertheless I can't draw my eyes away from the returned searches.

The web is strangely silent on James Berkeley. Besides his Wiki information page and official film pages, there isn't very much at all.

Obviously he keeps his private life to himself.

Guiltily, I scan down a few more pages. There is nothing to suggest he ever had a drug problem. But perhaps he's managed to hide it. It's not unheard of.

The only page I see which promises to divulge any personal information at all is an interview with a newspaper I've never heard of.

The headline of the search result is: *"James Berkeley and the Last Red Rose"*

I open the search and begin to read.

It's your usual director-interview, talking about his latest movie. Then something catches my eye.

The journalist questions James on the symbolism of roses in the film. I read on.

Berkeley tells me that roses have a special symbolism for him, reports the piece. *He tells me he has never given a red rose, since his mother died.*

I remember the yellow roses he bought me. Yellow for jealously, he said. So what do red symbolise? Love. The answer comes to me as obvious.

For some reason, I feel a deep and sad longing. I wonder if he'll ever buy red roses for me.

Serves you right for poking around in his personal life, I tell myself, allowing the wave of sadness to wash over me. I click shut the internet page determinedly, ashamed of myself for spying.

Then I turn to the bathroom sink and splash cold water on my face, resolving to pull myself together.

I decide I am determined to have a night out without thinking anymore about James. Taking one last look in the mirror, I head back out to the bar. My phone beeps in my pocket and I pull it out.

James. Typical. How does he do that?

I read the message.

I miss you gorgeous.

My heart melts and I push the phone back into my pocket, smiling. Ben can't be telling the truth. He just can't.

When I emerge back from the bathroom, I see that Sandy and Alex are clustered by the bar. I look in confusion to our table. Lorna and Ben are sat there, giggling and pawing at each other like teenagers with a bottle of Champagne on the table.

"What's up?" I ask, heading for where they're standing. "Why are you at the bar?"

Alex rolls his eyes and pushes his glasses a little further up the bridge of his nose.

"Ask the love birds," he says, with a bored wave towards the table. "He shows up with a bottle of fizz and suddenly they're all over each other. Me and Sandy thought we'd best give them some room, because they sure as hell should get one."

Sandy gives me a rueful smile, and I look back at the table. Lorna has a full glass of Champagne and I purse my lips.

"She's already had two glasses," says Sandy, following my line of gaze. "Does he know she's diabetic?"

"I don't know," I say. "Maybe Lorna hasn't told him. She does seem to like him a lot. Perhaps she's embarrassed."

Alex looks unconvinced and glares daggers at the table. Neither Lorna or Ben notice.

"We're heading to Camden," says Sandy. "Want to come with us?"

I shake my head, looking back at Lorna. "I should check that she's ok. We're supposed to be sharing a ride home."

Alex takes a final slug of the free cocktail. "Mr Fancy Pants said he has somewhere else he was going after here. Made it clear no one else was invited. Not even Lorna. I'd say when that bottle is done, you'll have your friend back."

"Ok," I say, wondering whether I should join the table.

"Sure you don't want to come with?" asks Sandy.

"No, that's ok."

Alex pats my arm. "You're a good friend."

"She'd do the same for me."

"Sweetheart, she wouldn't. But you're an angel for thinking it," Alex replies. He and Sandy give me a hug before heading out to take the underground to Camden.

After they leave, I flip open my phone.

There's a new message.

Are you ignoring me?

I smile and text back.

Not ignoring you. Out with friends in the Met Bar.

The truth is, I'm showing off a little by telling him I'm in the Met. I know James Berkeley can get in anywhere he wants, but I have my own ways of getting in the best places, even without him.

Almost instantly my phone beeps.

That's a relief. Wish you were here. Premieres with the wife are boring.

I give a half smile. I'm not sure I'm cool enough with his situation to be able to joke about it yet.

I toy with my phone wondering about what Ben told me. Not the kind of thing I can put in a text message.

My phone beeps again.

See you later?

See me later? When does he mean?

When? I type back.

Tonight? I'm only across the street. My after party is in St James Hotel.

I bite my lip. I didn't expect him to want to see me tonight. Or for him to be so nearby. To be honest, I've had as much emotion as I can take for a day. I need time to think. To work out what he wants from me.

I didn't realise he was only across the street though. The idea of him so close is tempting. But I set my mental resolve.

Not tonight. I write. *Tired.*

The phone beeps again.

Tomorrow?

I laugh. *You're persistent.* I tap.

There's a few minutes this time before my phone buzzes an answer.

Persistence is required for everything worth having in life. Pick you up at 8?

I smile to myself. He really is persistent.

Ok. I text.

I look back to the table where Ben and Lorna are sitting. Ben is nowhere to be seen. And Lorna… I suddenly see that Lorna is slumped forward, face down on the table.

My phone beeps again. But this time I don't reply, because I'm racing over to the table.

"Lorna?" She's out cold, her perfect features pressed against the black vinyl of the table. The phone in my pocket starts ringing but I ignore it.

"Lorna!" I pull her upright, looking about for help. I can't see any staff nearby and I don't want to leave her to run to the bar.

If her drink has been spiked, I won't leave her even for a second. Not after what happened to me.

"Wake up." I sit her upright, gently slapping at her cheeks. Her eyes flutter and I see they are rolled back in the sockets.

The phone rings again. I ignore it, trying to shake Lorna to consciousness. It cuts out and then starts ringing.

In desperate confusion I grab it out of my pocket and answer.

"I can't talk, my friend is ill," I yell into the phone, before cramming it back into my pocket without hanging up.

"Lorna!" I shout again. "Lorna. Please wake up!"

I look out into the wider bar area. It seems so alien to shout in this muted and elegant place. But I do anyway.

"Help!" I call to the bar. Across the hushed tones of conversation happening elsewhere, the barman doesn't hear me.

"Help!" I shout more loudly. "My friend is unconscious!"

This time it works, and the barman, alongside several drinkers, turn in anxious alarm. The barman is first on the scene, running to the table.

He's young, not much older than twenty, and already panicking.

"Did you call an ambulance?" he asks, seeing Lorna pale and out cold.

An ambulance. Of course. How stupid.

I pull out my phone and dial 999.

"Hold her," I say to the barman, as I stand to talk in the phone.

"Hello caller," says a voice at the other end. "What's your emergency?"

"Um. Medical," I say, my voice panicked. "My friend. She's diabetic and she might have drunk too much alcohol. I think she could be going into a diabetic coma."

"Where are you please?"

"The Met Bar. On St James Street."

"We're sending an ambulance now. Can you describe your friend's condition to me please?"

I look back to Lorna's beautiful face, and the tears start coming. "Um. She's not moving. She won't open her eyes," I start to sob. "She won't respond to her name."

"Ok, ma'am," says the voice on the other end. "We're sending someone for you now. Please keep calm and try to keep your friend conscious."

"She's not conscious!" I virtually scream the words in panic.

There's a beeping sound and I realise another caller is trying to get through on my phone. Berkeley. I ignore the beeping.

"Ok," I say. "Is there anything else I can do?"

"The ambulance is less than two minutes away," says the voice. "Do your best to talk to her, get through to her."

"Has she taken anything?" says a deep voice by my side. I turn in amazement to see Berkeley.

"How did you get here so fast?" I am momentarily rail-roaded by his sudden appearance.

"I ran. Has she taken anything?"

The question throws me.

"What? I. Um. No, I don't think so."

Lorna's eyes flutter a little, and I seize on the gesture, shaking her. She groans.

"You're sure she hasn't taken anything?" James's eyes are searching my face, and there is something in them I've never seen before. As though a tiny part of him is unsure, frightened.

The memory of Ben's words comes back. *Berkeley has a problem with drugs.*

I push it away. I have more serious concerns.

"Yes. I'm sure. She's diabetic. She's had alcohol and she shouldn't."

The unfamiliar expression on his face vanishes. Lorna is blinking a little now, and starting to move groggily.

I feel a rush of relief.

"She needs sugar. Now." James looks around until he sees the barman.

"You have sugar syrup behind the bar and sliced oranges," Berkeley is saying. "Bring a bottle and some slices. Quickly."

The barman pauses for a moment.

"I'm not ordering a drink man," growls Berkeley. "This girl needs sugar. Get syrup and orange slices. Now!"

The barman runs off, leaving me to stare up at the surprise arrival.

"She wasn't conscious," I manage, my lip trembling as Lorna becomes slowly more lifelike, twisting her head around a little on the vinyl table.

"How much has she drunk?"

"I… I don't know."

"Was she buying her own drinks?"

"No… I…"

"Someone was buying them? How many?"

This focuses my mind.

"I… Uh. It was a bottle of Champagne," I look at the table.

"Two glasses on the table," he says. "The most she could have had from that bottle would be three. Champagne bottles only hold four. Most likely she's had two or less."

His calm assessment helps quell my rising panic. It is such a relief to have someone who knows what to do.

The barman has returned, uncertainly clutching a bottle of sugar syrup.

In my panic, I had forgotten all this. But now it's all flooding back to me.

Of course. I've known this for years. Better, probably, than Lorna herself. Alcohol lowers blood sugar, which can lead to fainting. She needs a quick fix of something sweet.

The sugar syrup comes with a speed pourer for easy shots into cocktails. I would never have thought of that.

Berkeley lowers the metal spout into the side of Lorna's mouth and administers a trickle of sticky liquid.

He tilts her head back.

"It should be absorbed by the back of her tongue," he's saying. "It doesn't matter if she doesn't swallow it."

There's a tense few seconds, and then Lorna groggily opens her eyes properly, and gulps down the syrup.

She stares up at James.

For a moment, she blinks comically, trying to figure out how she woke up staring into the face of a famous movie director. Then she gives a little shudder and looks around.

"What happened?" she mumbles, her words slurred.

"Here," says James, handing her the orange slices. "Suck on these."

She allows him to push the first slice into her mouth, and I feel a flash of jealously.

Then I hear the sirens outside.

"The ambulance!"

"I don't need an ambulance," says Lorna, looking confused. "I'm fine. Really." She rubs her forehead with her hand. "I shouldn't have had so much Champagne," she admits.

"It's better she goes out to the ambulance," says James, "just so they can check her out."

I nod, feeling exhausted suddenly. "I'll go with her," I say.

"No," says James, "you get her coat and purse. I'll carry her out."

James leans into the booth and lifts Lorna's long limbs with ease. I feel another stab of jealousy, seeing her in his arms.

I busy myself collecting Lorna's coat and purse from the cloak room. No easy task when her ticket is somewhere on her person. Likely in her bra, knowing Lorna. But the barman comes to my aid, and the reluctant cloakroom attendant relinquishes her fur coat and designer purse.

I gather them up and turn to leave. But now James is back inside the bar.

"She's fine," he says. "The ambulance crew say she doesn't need to be admitted to hospital. They took her blood sugar levels and tested her pupil contraction and said she's in good health. Though they said it's better she goes home early."

"Where is she?"

"Sitting outside smoking a cigarette. She came around pretty fast after the sugar."

I nod my thanks and turn to head outside, but James grabs my arm.

"I can't come outside with you," he says, "there's paparazzi all over the place, and I won't risk your face in the papers again. But I'll be waiting here, if you'd like to come back and have a drink with me."

"I... I don't know," I say. "I think I might need to make sure Lorna gets home ok."

He nods. "I understand completely. But I'll be here waiting for you if you change your mind."

I rush outside to find Lorna is, as James said, sat on a step smoking a cigarette. Lorna doesn't smoke, but she occasionally has a few puffs if she's getting tired on a big night out. She looks as though nothing has happened and gives me a wide grin as I join her.

"Where's the ambulance?" I say, looking about in confusion. I expected it to be chaos out here.

"They went pretty quick," says Lorna, blowing out a column of smoke. "I was fine really, as soon as the sugar syrup hit my mouth. But I couldn't miss the chance to be carried out by Mr James Berkeley now, could I?"

She gives me an impish grin, and I laugh in relief. I'm so glad she's alright, she could say almost anything right now and I'd forgive her.

"He's quite a guy," she says wistfully.

I nod at the truth of this.

"I wasn't so sure about him at first," she continues, "after that thing with the taxi and Ben. But I've changed my mind. He's your regular knight in shining armour isn't he? How did he even get here so fast?"

"He was only a few doors down in another bar."

Lorna nods. "Makes sense. All the big premiere parties are in this part of town."

"So shall we grab a cab, Lorna? I've got your coat and purse." I wave away a plume of her smoke, and she respectfully drops the cigarette and grinds it out.

"You're not going back inside to see Berkeley?" She sounds surprised.

I shake my head.

"Of course not. My best friend fainted tonight. Admittedly through her own stupid actions," I add, waggling a finger at her. "But there's no way I'm letting you home alone."

"And there's no way I'm ruining the rest of your evening," says Lorna. "Honestly, honey. I'm *fine*. More than fine."

She stands and does a little energetic dance on the spot.

"See? I'm even thinking of heading over to Camden to party."

I laugh, dragging her back down to sitting. She clearly is restored to health.

"No way," I admonish. "You're not going out partying, Lorna Hamilton. You are going straight home to bed."

"Yes, mum," Lorna mock salutes, and then her face turns serious. "I would never forgive myself if I ruined any more of your night on my account. So just do me a favour, ok. Stay and have a drink with Mr Rescue. It's the least he deserves."

"Lorna. I'm not sure about that."

"Well you might as well get sure. Cause if you don't let me get a cab home by myself, I'm not doing washing up for a month. And you know how that would bug you."

I mock sigh and smile at her. Staying for a drink with James *is* tempting. I'd been so sure I should stay away. But seeing him in person… I'm not sure I have the strength to leave him sitting alone in the bar. Not when Lorna is clearly in such good health.

"Ok…" I say, "maybe just one drink. But you call me when you get home to say you arrived safe."

"Atta girl!" Lorna slaps me on the back.

"Promise you'll call. And I'm seeing you directly into a cab first."

Lorna rolls her eyes. "Ok, fine. But it's really not necessary. And that poor hot guy is waiting in there all alone. Someone else might get to him before you do."

Chapter 19

Having seen Lorna safely into a black cab, I head back into the Met Bar. The glittering décor has taken on a new look now I know Berkeley is in here. It seems more sensuous and decadent.

But as I enter the main bar, there is no sign of him.

Lorna's words come back to me – *someone else might get to him before you do.*

I dismiss the unwelcome thought, but it still brings with it a flash of jealously. I wonder if I can get through all these emotions which this situation is causing. I feel as though my heart might explode if I'm subjected to much more, and it's been less than a week since we met.

Then I remember Berkeley saying that I should be taken in hand. Is that what he means? Freedom from all these thoughts? All this energy trying to work out what he wants with me? Maybe I should just trust and let go.

I smile to myself, resolving he'll never hear me say that out loud.

Then I see a single rose on the table where Lorna and I were sitting. I move towards it, wondering if it was left for Lorna by Ben.

The bloom is orange rather than red. An unusual choice for romance. And it's also perfect, I see, as I pick it up from the table. Every crisp petal is flawless.

There is a cream card underneath and I flip it over.

Isabella, says the familiar writing. My heart skips in my chest.

Orange is for passion. Join me in room 9.

Oh no. He got a room? Orange for passion? The message brings a thrill of anticipation and anxiety all in one.

It's yet another cryptic flower bouquet from Berkeley. The last roses he bought me signified jealousy. These mean passion. So I suppose I should be grateful for the improvement.

I call to mind the newspaper article. *He has never given a red rose since the death of his mother.*

Is he making a point? That our relationship is not about love?

I shake the thought away, returning to the situation in hand.

Joining him a hotel room. That wasn't part of the deal.

My phone beeps and I look down distractedly. It's from Lorna.

Got home safe.

I smile and ring her number.

She answers immediately.

"Get off the phone, Isabella Green, and stop worrying about me."

I laugh.

"Ok, fine. But you really are ok? You don't need me to come back?"

"And tuck me into bed? Purlease, Issy. I'm fine. I told you. I'll watch a movie and go to bed. Scout's honour."

"Ok."

We both hang up, and I return to considering the perfect orange rose in my hand.

Flipping to the message screen I begin writing a text. This time, to James Berkeley.

Your room? That wasn't the arrangement.

Almost immediately the phone beeps.

Forgive my discourtesy. We cannot be seen together in public. This is for your protection.

So. The old issue of the press and Madison. I purse my lips. My phone beeps again.

You can be assured that as a gentleman I will take no more freedoms than I would in an open bar.

I smile at this. Then I text back.

So formal Mr Berkeley. And what if I wanted to take freedoms with you?

There. That will give him something to think about.

There's a pause. Then a message appears.

I am open to negotiation.

I toy with my phone, wondering what to do. He has, after all, changed the rules. We were supposed to be having a drink in a bar. A room in a hotel is very different. And I'm still reeling from what Ben Gracey told me. That James has a drug problem.

I begin tapping out a message.

I am not sure you're playing fair.

"I have no intention of playing fair," says a deep voice at my shoulder. I jump, halfway to sending the message, and see James standing right behind me.

His cheek is almost against mine, and he wraps his arms around me from behind and eases me phone from my hand.

"Better we do without this," he murmurs. "It seems to make you even more rebellious than usual."

"We were supposed to be meeting in the bar," I say stubbornly. But my body is pressing back into his, relaxing into the strength of his arms.

He turns me around to face him.

"Isabella, I have explained to you the situation. Things with Madison are currently in flux. Until then, we cannot be seen together in public."

"Then why are you here?"

"I realised that it wasn't gentlemanly to expect you to find the room by yourself," he concedes. "So I have come to escort you personally."

He takes my arm firmly in his.

"And I don't expect to find any resistance."

Before I have a chance to protest, he walks me across the bar and into the sumptuous carpeted corridors of the Metropolitan Hotel.

"It's not far," he murmurs in my ear as we turn a corner. "I am always sure to get a room a convenient distance away."

And with the highest price tag, I think to myself, wondering what a last minute room at the Metropolitan would have cost.

I find my legs are betraying me, and I follow him without a word to the door of his room.

"Here we are," he says, opening the door and gesturing I should walk in first.

"This isn't my usual choice of hotel," he adds, as I'm greeted by a vision in deep purple carpets and an enormous bed decked in sumptuous deep white bed linen and designer pillows.

"Oh?" I say, trying to keep the wonder on my face in check.

"I like hotels with a little more boutique about them," he explains, shutting the door behind him. "Places which feel more intimate."

He's standing facing me now, his lips only inches from mine.

"You made me a promise," I say in a quavering voice, trying not to react to his proximity. I am determined to question him about the drug issue.

"Oh yes?" he leans closer.

"That you would treat me the same here as you would in an open bar."

"Well, I have a confession to make, Isabella," he says. "I don't always keep my promises. At least not where you're concerned."

He takes my chin softly in his hands and begins planting gentle kisses over my face. I close my eyes as his lips brush my cheeks, my eyelids. The delicate feeling of his lips awakes something deep inside me.

I swallow and feel myself yielding to him. A dangerous little voice in my head makes a suggestion. *Even if he did have a drug problem, what would I do about it?*

"We should talk," I manage, my voice betraying my true feelings.

"Oh yes?" he continues kissing me, moving his mouth down the side of my neck. The sensation is electric, as though he's raising every hair on by body with his touch.

His mouth moves further down, planting soft kisses across my collar bone. I feel my neck arch back, my eyes fluttering.

"I need to know something," I protest, as his mouth continues to work on my body. He loosens the top of my dress, and his lips begin kissing the tops of my breasts.

"What do you want to know?" The words are partially lost.

"I saw Ben Gracey today."

"Oh."

James's head comes up. His green eyes still have a softness about them. But they are wary too.

Is this confirmation that Ben was telling the truth?

"He. Um. He said some things," I manage.

"He always does," says James sardonically. He's upright facing me now, and he sighs. "Come and sit down, Isabella," he says. "Perhaps we should have that drink after all."

Part of me feels as though I've disappointed him. But I hold firm. I am entitled to know, I think, something about him. Particularly since his behaviour is so erratic.

I sit on a white couch, and James opens the mini bar. It is stacked full of glittering miniature versions of branded spirits, French wine and Champagne.

"Would you like a gin and tonic?" he says. "Or shall I order a drink to be delivered from the bar."

"Gin and tonic is fine," I say, watching as his hands work to slice and squeeze lime, and measure gin, ice and tonic.

"You look very professional," I say.

He gives a half smile. "I've made myself adept in most drinks services," he says. "It helps immeasurably in having an understanding of when drinks are made well."

I like that, I decide, that he's actually learned something menial despite his vast wealth. He walks towards me holding two clinking glasses of ice and lime, and hands me one.

I take a grateful sip. The gin is sour, complex, and is perfectly balanced by the fresh lime and sparkling tonic.

"Thank you."

"My pleasure. Now," he sits next to me on the couch, so our knees are touching. "What is it that Ben Gracey has been telling you?"

He says it in a world-weary kind of way, and I wonder again if I've misjudged him.

"He… Um. He said you'd had a problem with drugs," I say, raising my eyes to him in apology for even partially crediting such a silly story. But he doesn't meet my gaze.

"That's true," he says finally.

There's a long pause whilst we both consider this. I remember that strange look on his face earlier in the bar, when he asked me if Lorna had taken anything.

"Do you still have a problem now?" I ask.

"No." He says this adamantly, meeting my gaze. "No, I do not. Nor will I be anywhere near where people are taking drugs. And I have a zero tolerance for actors who indulge. They are removed from set and asked to provide a weekly urine sample until I can assure myself they are free from the habit."

"Ok." That makes sense, I think. Although it's typical controlling Berkeley.

"Is that why…"

The question is half-formed and James answers the unsaid words.

"Is that why I feel the need to be in control? Yes. Partially."

"Is it why you want me to be obedient to you? Because you have a problem with control?" I am surprised at my courage for saying the words out loud.

James seems surprised too. He looks down for a moment, considering, and then meets my gaze.

"In a way. Yes."

He leans forward and takes my hands.

"I have something of an addictive nature, Isabella." He's saying this almost apologetically. "My nature something I've battled with, to an extent, and overcome. I have not had the easiest of lives, and I am drawn to activities which allow me to forget. To immerse myself. At one time this was drugs."

Practices that allow him to forget. Like beating women?

"So, what is it now?" I ask, my voice trembling.

"I… I like to give pleasure to others," he says. "But my background has drawn out my preferences in a single direction."

He meets my gaze, his green eyes open and honest.

"Creating submission," he says, "in those who desire it. This is what now allows me to lose myself. To forget my demons."

I open my mouth to say something and James places a finger over my lips.

"I have told you all I am willing to explain," he says. "I don't want you to ask me anything else."

I take a nervous sip of my gin and tonic, wondering what to say now.

"What if I can help you?" I say finally.

"What do you mean?"

"What if I can help you? In a different way?"

"How?" his eyes are alert, wary.

I swallow my mouthful of gin. "What if someone could help you by truly caring for you?" My words come out as a soft whisper. I think for a terrible moment that he might laugh at me, or dismiss the idea. But instead he looks thoughtful.

"I don't know, Isabella." James shakes his head. "I think it might be too late to change me now."

"Then what if I were willing to try it your way?" My jaw sets slightly as I say the words. But really I'm in too deep. I'm falling hard for this complicated, powerful man. I'm under his spell, and I am prepared to give more of myself than I thought possible.

"You don't know what you're suggesting," he says. His voice is dangerous.

"So show me."

The words come out thickly, and without meaning to, I find myself pouting my lips as I say them.

"You're sure?"

I blink. "Yes. I want to know what you mean."

There is a long pause, and for a moment, I think he will refuse.

Then he nods, slowly, not taking his eyes from mine.

"Very well," he says.

I stare back at him.

"For the next hour you are mine to do as I will with, do you understand?"

I swallow, not sure whether I can agree.

"You will do whatever is asked of you without question. And I, for my part, promise that I will not do anything you will not like."

That doesn't sound so bad.

"However," adds James with an unfathomable smile, "you may not realise you like some of the things I plan to do to you. Do you accept?"

I try to imagine what he could mean by that, and find I can't.

It's as though I'm at a crossroads. One way headed for the tame and empty life I've always known. The other branching out to something which is unknown and frightening. In my heart I already know which path I'm bound to choose.

I find myself nodding. Mostly, I think, I just want to know. If it's really bad then I still have an outside chance of escaping with my heart intact. But if I continue to let myself get ever more entangled in the complicated wonder of James Berkeley, then I may never get out.

James stands suddenly and looks over me for a long moment. Then, very gently, he loosens the orange rose from my grip. I didn't realise until this moment that I was still holding it.

"Wait there," he says.

He walks into the bathroom, and I hear taps running. I sit squirming on my seat, wondering what he has in mind for me.

He appears again at the bathroom door.

"You will find a black box on top of the mini-bar," he says. "Bring it into the bathroom. Do not open it."

He vanishes again, and I blink, standing to obey his instructions. So far, not so bad. What does he have planned for me in the bathroom?

I approach the mini-bar and see there is a slim black box sat atop. Next to it are a set of beautifully wrapped chocolates.

I lift the box, and can see there is white writing on the top of it. *"Intimacy Kit"* is printed in delicate white looping text.

Did James bring this with him? My eyes flick to a tiny menu propped up by the mini-bar. It lists the prices of all the spirits and Champagne inside. Then I see, at the end, 'Kiki de Montparnasse Intimacy Kit" is listed, with a price of £225.

I walk into the bathroom, carrying the box, wondering what's inside. Since it's supplied by the hotel, there can't be anything too frightening inside.

As I enter, a cloud of fragrant steam welcomes me. James has run a bath, and floating on top are the petals of the orange rose.

The bath is absolutely enormous, with a large antique style gold-plated tap which also runs to an elaborate showerhead. There is also a large shower in the bathroom and two his-and-her sinks, with the same style gold taps as the bath. There are mirrors everywhere.

He picks up a bottle of elegant looking bath oil – another payable extra of the room I assume – and tips a thin stream into the water.

"I have chosen oil instead of bubbles," he says. "I want to see every part of your naked body in this tub. And the oil will also help for what I have in mind for you."

Oh. What does he have in mind?

"I assume it's against the rules for me to ask what you are going to do to me?"

I'm standing in the entrance, holding the black box nervously.

James smiles slightly.

"We make the rules together, Isabella," he says. "But for the purposes of this experiment. No. You are not permitted to ask."

He nods at me. "Open the box."

Taking a step closer I loosen the lid. Inside is pink and black tissue paper, stuck with a single round label, bearing the words "Kiki de Montparnasse."

I pull open the paper, tearing it softly. Underneath is a beautiful lace G-string. I lift it from the box. It is made so delicately, it almost feels as though it will fall apart in my hands.

"Take out the rest," James commands.

I delve inside again and bring out a tiny black vibrator. It feels soft. Like velvety skin. There are also condoms and lubricant.

"Put the condoms and the lubricant on the side," he says, gesturing to the place where the soaps and shampoos are elegantly stacked.

I do as he asks.

"Give the vibrator to me."

I walk towards him and push the black vibrator into his outstretched hand. His fingers close around it.

"A small advantage of this hotel," he notes as he takes it. "This particular lingerie brand is one of my favourites. I look forward to taking you to one of their stores soon. They sell all manner of interesting items."

I can tell by the way he says interesting items that he's not talking about underwear.

"Now," he says, "undress, and put on the panties which were in the box."

I hesitate for a moment.

"Isabella," he says sternly. "You agreed to try things my way."

I nod and begin removing my clothes. He watches as I unzip my retro print dress at the side and let it fall to the floor.

I'm wearing black underwear. Not the designer kind I imagine he's used to. But it's one of my better sets.

"Nice." He stands, looking me up and down. "Now take it off."

I pause fractionally, but before he can say anything, I unhook my bra and let it fall to the floor. Then I slide off my panties.

This last step is about as much as I can bear of him looking at me, and I almost race to grab a towel to cover myself up.

"I want you to stay there for a moment, Isabella," he says, "and let me look at you."

I was dreading he'd ask this. Standing naked in front of a man pulls up every bad thought I ever had about my body. And not even to be wearing panties. I feel the flush sweep from my chest up over my face.

"You are very beautiful," says James. "Under my care you will learn to believe it."

He takes a step forward and I hear a faint buzzing sound. He moves his hand to touch my nipples, and I see the vibrator in his hand.

He reaches forward and touches the end of it very gently to the edge of my nipple, making it instantly erect.

"Ahhhh," I can't help myself from sighing out. My body is so ready for him. I feel myself pushing my breasts forward, wanting more.

He rolls the vibrator expertly around the nipple, teasing it out, and then moves it to the other side. Both my nipples are rock hard and tingling. My breasts are alive with sensation and I feel a pulse of warmth between my legs.

James steps back, silencing the vibrator, and considers me again for a moment.

I stand, panting a little, with my lips parted. My nipples, I am aware, are deep pink and jutting forward.

James lets his eyes roam my naked body. I still feel self-conscious, but the rising lust has helped quell some of my embarrassment.

"Now," he says, "put on the panties which came with the kit."

He doesn't need to ask twice. I pick them up, relieved to have the chance to cover my lower half.

Carefully, I work the delicate lace up and through each leg. The panties feel soft against my skin, decadent. I tug them over my behind. The strap falls in-between my buttocks in a surprisingly comfortable way.

I've never worn a G-string, and it makes me feel scandalous. Like a different woman. The shape of the open panties at the back also makes me doubly conscious of my naked behind. But in a good way. I've never felt so sexy in my life.

"Come over here," says James, "and get into the tub."

I open my mouth to remind him that I'm still wearing underwear. And then I catch his expression and close it again.

Slowly, I make my way towards the tub. Then I raise one leg after the other, placing myself standing into the water, with my hips rolling to emphasise my skimpily clad behind.

"Easy, Isabella," he murmurs. "I don't want to fuck you too soon."

I turn to face him.

"What if I want you too?"

My eyes are challenging.

I see him swallow.

"Lower yourself into the water and bend over the side of the bath, facing away from me" he says.

I let my knees bend, sinking down into the warm water. Then I let my upper body slide forward, bending myself over the tub so that my behind is slightly raised, pointing in his direction. I feel vulnerable, but my curiosity is also heightened.

"Bend further forwards," he says, "I am going to give you a little of that spanking you have been asking for."

Now it's my turn to swallow. What have I got myself in for?

I feel his hand scoop into the water behind me and splash my behind with water, soaking the G-string.

The fabric clings to me wetly, like a second skin.

"The water is to raise sensitivity," he explains, leaning forward to caress my buttock with his wet hand.

He kneels onto the floor outside the bathtub. Then he reaches a hand forward and tugs my head around by a handful of hair, so I am facing him. I see his other hand, poised to strike my naked behind. James looks straight into my eyes.

"Are you sure you want this?" he asks.

His words from earlier flash through me. That he seeks out things to forget the demons from his past. Could we ever work?

I close my eyes. Only one way to find out.

"Yes," I say, opening them and meeting his gaze.

His hand strokes across my buttocks again, caressing. His slides a finger slightly between them, running it along the crevasse.

Then he lifts his hand and lets it fall, sharply, against the skin.

Oh.

The slap of his hand combined with the water on my skin brings a jolt of electric sensation. It's not painful, and this surprises me.

He spanks me again, letting his hand fall firmly against the skin.

I gasp as a jolt of lust shudders through me. The flat of his hand on my buttock stings, but it brings pleasure rather than pain. As though this area of my body is being woken up.

James slaps my behind for a third time, and then slides his fingers down, between my buttocks and further forward, tucking them beneath the G-string to where I am already growing wet.

"You don't seem to find the idea of submitting to me so unpleasant," he whispers. "Perhaps you simply needed to discover what it means for yourself."

James spanks again, a little harder, and this time it's only just not painful.

"Now," he whispers, staring into my face. "It is time for you to satisfy me."

He stands and moves around the other side of the bathtub, so his waist is just above my head. I realise I am staring straight into the zip of his trousers. The bulge of his erection is almost against my face.

I lean forward and nuzzle at him, raising my behind in the bathtub.

"Oh God, Isabella," his hand strokes at my buttocks. "You have no idea how good you look in that underwear. Or what I want to do to you in it."

His other hand comes down and frees his erection from his trousers.

He grabs a fistful of my hair tightly and manoeuvres my head forward.

"Open your mouth," he gasps, pushing himself forward against my face.

I let my lips part and he slides inside and towards the back of my throat, groaning with pleasure.

I let my tongue range around, sliding under the head and up the shaft of his penis.

He relinquishes his grip on my hair, lost in the sensation, and I realise in a sudden burst of power that I am the one in control now.

I reach a hand up out of the water and slide it between his legs, letting it run softly where his penis meets his body.

He lets out another moan, and I feel his body tense.

"Steady," he groans, "you'll make me come in your mouth."

Suddenly, this is what I want more than anything. And I increase the pressure with my hand, and take him deeper into my mouth, using my tongue to stroke and stimulate him.

"Isabella…" he gasps. But I move forward again, keeping the pace with my mouth and stroking with my hand. I am giddy with my ability to control him, to make him do what I want.

I tighten my lips and feel a fluttering begin, near the head of his penis. He is close, I realise. He tries to pull away, but I won't let him. I dig both hands into his buttocks to push him more firmly into my mouth.

This tips him over the edge, and he ejaculates in a shuddering spasm, moaning aloud as the waves of salty fluid leave his body.

I swallow, noticing how he tastes, how he submits utterly to the pleasure. And then I let him slide out of my mouth, and stare up at him, from my position in the rose-strewn bathtub.

"Isabella," he murmurs, looking down at me. "Where did you learn to do that?"

I smile up at him, pleased with myself.

"Female intuition," I say.

He looks into my face for a moment, as if deciding something.

"Turn around," he says after a moment. "I think it's my turn to teach you something."

He's back into dominant mode, I realise, wondering if I should submit again this time.

"Turn around," he commands again, and I realise there's no disobeying him.

I twist so I am on all fours in the bathtub, and hear him undress behind me. In a moment he plunges into the warm water, positioning himself behind, between my legs.

"Have you ever pleasured yourself with a shower head?" he asks.

I shake my head. "No."

"You should try it," he says, "I hear many women find it very enjoyable." There is a little humour in his voice, but without seeing his face, I find it hard to read.

Then he leans over and unhooks the showerhead.

"Now you will find out what the sensation is like when another person uses it on you," he says.

Oh.

He turns on the water, and I feel myself growing warm, responding to the idea. I've never had water run over me like that, and I don't know what it will feel like.

He adjusts the taps and takes a moment getting the temperature right.

"We want to be sure to give you the maximum sensation," he is saying.

Then the shower water is running over my naked behind, where it is raised up out of the water.

The sensation is complex. It's erotic, yet unfamiliar at the same time. But the warm water tunnelling between my legs is making me wild with pleasure.

James hooks his finger under the wet G-string where it rests in between my buttocks.

"Now," he says, "I am going to teach you a new sensation. I am going to make you come, Isabella, and I am also going to stimulate you anally."

Wait. Anally?

I tense, uncertain whether I can agree to this. I agreed to his terms, but I'm not sure I feel comfortable with what he might be suggesting.

But he is sliding his thumb up and down, under the G-string, in the crevasse of my ass, and I realise I don't want him to stop doing it.

I shake my head, caught between the heavenly-sexy feeling of where his thumb is stroking, and the idea of any kind of anal act.

"Do you like what I'm doing now?" he asks softly, letting his thumb drop deeper towards the centre of my ass.

I flinch at the sensation of where his thumb is. But I can't lie to him.

"Yes…" I stutter, "But…"

"But you've never had anything inside your ass? You don't like the idea of it?"

He says the words silkily, in a low voice. How can he make everything sound so sexy?

"Yes. I mean, no. I don't like the idea of it," I gasp as his thumb begins to circle inside the crevasse, seeking out the centre.

"Isabella, what I am doing now is not to do with sub-ordinance. This is about pleasure," he whispers. "I am going to pleasure you here, and you are going to like it."

He drops the showerhead, so the spray hits further down between my legs, and I moan aloud in pleasure.

The warm water pelting against me is unbearably sensual.

He leans in towards my ear, his thumb still circling dangerously inside my buttocks.

"Open your legs wider."

Still on all fours, I spread my legs slightly, so they are pressed against the sides of the large bath.

I hear him rip open a condom and roll it on.

Then he moves the showerhead closer, onto the area I've just exposed by opening my legs. The feeling is exquisite. Almost too much.

I feel his thumb enter my ass, just a fraction. A confusing mix of emotions hit my brain. I can't deny it feels good. Part of me wants him to go deeper. More. But it's all so alien to have stimulation where he's moving his hand. Just the idea of where his fingers are feels too wrong.

"Do you like that?" he asks.

"I don't know," I admit. "In my head it feels wrong."

"And yet, your body…" James circles his thumb, pushing it a little further in. "I can feel by the way you are tensing around my fingers. Your body likes this."

I gasp again, as another jolt of pleasure drives through me. He's right, damn him. I do like what he's doing to me.

"Let go of what's happening in your head, Isabella," he whispers. "Let your body decide what it wants."

He moves the tumbling water of the shower even closer between my legs, driving against me, bringing me ever closer to orgasm.

Keeping the warm water running tight against me, James leans across me and presses a button on the bath.

Immediately, a froth of bubbles and foam start up from the bottom of the tub. It's a Jacuzzi bath, I realise, and the onslaught of moving water hits my sensitised skin like a barrage.

"Oh God," I moan, feeling the moving water against me at every angle. With the showerhead making its relentless stimulation, I feel myself building closer to orgasm.

The water has risen to cover most of my ass now, but in the enormous tub, it's still a long way from over-flowing. Golden feelings are sweeping up my legs and through my body.

Then James slips a whole finger into my ass, and I feel him circle it gently inside of me and then push it firmly back and forth.

"Ahhh!" the sensation is almost too much. It's glorious, but shameful at the same time. He's fucking my ass with his finger now, moving expertly in and out.

It feels so wrong to have someone's fingers there. But the feeling is so good, I can't help myself. I rock back and forward, urging him as he begins plunging his finger in faster, back and forth.

"The oil in the tub is helping to keep you open to me," he whispers. "In a moment, I'm going to move the shower head against your clitoris. From the flush on your body, and the shuddering in your thighs, I would judge it will bring you to orgasm in a few seconds."

I nod, arrested with the sensation of him in my ass, and the showerhead pressure on me.

"But first," he whispers, "I am going to put another finger inside your ass-hole. Do I have your permission to do that?"

As he says the words, he circles his finger inside my ass, pushing it all the way in, and creating a deep feeling of penetration. He moves the showerhead closer to my clitoris.

I gasp, unable to refuse him. And I realise that I want more. More of him inside me.

"Yes," I moan. "Put your fingers in my ass."

"You have no idea how sexy it is to hear you say that, Isabella," he whispers. And then he moves the showerhead so the water pressure is now running directly over my clitoris.

I feel the orgasm hit almost immediately, and as it does, James slides another finger inside my ass.

I reach my peak, the orgasm exploding hotly between my legs and out across my entire body. It shudders through me, pulsing pleasure into every part.

I feel James's fingers and my ass tightens around them as I come. Then suddenly, he begins to move them, firmly, fast, pulsing his fingers in and out quickly.

Keeping his fingers working my ass, he positions himself between my legs. Then with a strong push, he forces into me, stretching me open and filling me up.

Then he is fucking me from behind, plunging deep into where I am already pulsing with orgasm.

His fingers fuck my ass as he slams into me with his body. He moves hard, urgently, and I feel the aftershock of my orgasm begin to build higher.

"Oh God, Isabella," he moans. "I'm going to come."

And then his fingers plunge deep into my ass as he explodes inside of me.

In the still shuddering aftermath of my first orgasm comes another wave, shattering through me in a second intense bolt of pleasure. I am coming for a second time.

The orgasm, it hits me with double force, and I cry out aloud.

Then the waves ripple slowly back, and I find my body collapsing, relaxing with the force of it.

James slides himself out of me, and flips me around in the tub.

It's all I can do not to sink under the water. I feel as though every need I ever had has just been sated.

I gaze up at him, hazily, my eyes in soft focus.

"Do you see Isabella," he says, "how if you trust in me I can give your greater pleasure?"

"Yes," I whisper, staring into his green eyes. In the after-light of the multiple orgasm he's just given me, they seem more beautiful than I've ever seen them before.

He smiles at me, a happy, boyish smile.

"I like making you come," he says. "You look so lovely, lying there in the water. And knowing that I've satisfied you makes me immensely happy."

I smile back at him and sit up so we're facing. He holds my hips with his hands.

"So tell me," I say, "did that take your mind off these demons of yours?"

It's a risky thing to say, I know, but to my relief he throws his head back and laughs.

"Yes," he says, when his amusement has subsided. "Very clever, Miss Green. You are quite right. When I'm with you, perhaps those demons are not so near."

He gazes at me for a moment, happy, but somehow calculating something. Then he rises to his feet and hands me a huge fluffy bathrobe.

"Come to bed," he says. "Perhaps we can find some other ways to chase away both of our demons."

Chapter 20

We float into the bed, and lay for a time in each other's arms.

Then, under the hotel sheets, James and I make love, our eyes locked, breathing perfectly into one another.

The softness of his movements opens up something different inside of me. And this time as he strokes me to orgasm with his body and his fingers, the climax feels different, deeper.

We fade into each other, tired and happy. And I realise with a falling feeling that there is no way back for me now. I am undeniable, irrevocably, in love with James Berkeley. The idea is frightening and exciting all at once.

I fall asleep in the soft scented sheets of the bed, but am woken later in the night by shouts. I turn to see James is twisting in his sleep, crying out aloud. I draw him tighter, and whisper him softly awake.

"James. You're having a nightmare."

The moment he wakes up, he looks glassy-eyed, confused, as though he doesn't know where he is.

"It's cold here," he says. His voice is sad, fearful, like a small boy.

"Shhh," I pull him close. "It's ok now, you had a bad dream."

He turns, and looks confused. The he blinks himself more awake.

"What happened?" he asks in more of his usual voice.

"You had a nightmare," I say. "You were crying out in your sleep."

"Oh."

He looks thoughtful.

"That happens sometimes. I didn't realise I spoke in my sleep. I apologise for waking you."

"Don't be silly." I'm staring at him. "Are you ok? It sounded like a really bad dream. You said it was cold," I add, hoping to jog his memory.

He shakes his head, as though trying to shrug an image from his head.

"It was nothing," he says. "Just a dream about when I was younger. Go back to sleep, Issy."

I lie back, and as I begin falling back to sleep, I feel him slip from the sheets and walk away from the bed.

The mysterious James Berkeley, my subconscious murmurs as the dreamy world takes over my thoughts. *Will I ever understand him?*

Then sleep takes over, and I fall into a place halfway between this hotel bedroom and somewhere different entirely.

In my dreams, a green-eyed boy in boarding-school uniform sits shivering. He asks me over and over when he can go home.

I wake to bright daylight, and my phone ringing by my ear. James is nowhere to be seen, and I grab the phone off the bedside table.

My mother's name flashes on the display. I realise I've not spoken to her in a few days. She probably wants to remind me of her impending visit.

"Hi, Mami."

"Morning, *carina*. Where are you?"

"I... Um. I'm at a friends," I manage. I'm not quite ready to explain the complexity of James Berkeley to my mother just yet.

"*Oooooh* I see." My mother can always tell when I'm hiding something. "Well, alright then darling. But are we still good to meet up in an hour?"

An hour?

"Don't tell me you forgot? I sent you an email." She sounds more amused than annoyed.

"I... I'm so sorry, Mami. I did forget. We organised it a few days ago, and it's been mad since then."

My mother gives her big, warm laugh.

"No problem, darling. I am not offended. I would rather you had a life, eh? Not holed up reading scripts or whatever you do. Or checking for emails from your mother." She laughs again.

I roll my eyes. My mother is always on me to have more of a social life.

"So you can tell me all about this *friend* later?" I can hear the curiosity in her voice.

"I... Um. Yeah. Sure, Mami."

"Do you want to meet a little later than we planned?"

I mentally calculate my position in London. I'm in Mayfair. We always meet in Trafalgar Square. It's a tradition since I moved to London.

"No, that's ok, Mami. I'm in Mayfair. It will only take me twenty minutes to walk to Trafalgar Square."

"Lovely. Ok then darling. Well I'm very excited. We go to the gallery, then we go to lunch and you tell me all about this friend of yours."

"Ok, Mami." I sigh, wondering how I'm going to explain things. I never could lie to my mother.

"And don't sigh, darling. We have nice day. Oh, I nearly forgot. I arrange to meet Robin and Carol for lunch too."

Robin and Carol are my aunt and uncle on my father's side. They live in a London suburb, and I stayed with them during my years at drama school.

I hated the long commute into central London on the underground, but I always loved Robin and Carol. They had no children of their own, and always treated me like a daughter.

We had a running joke that they had adopted me, and it was more or less true.

"Great idea, Mami," I say. "I should have remembered to invite them myself."

I realise it's been a few weeks since I went to see my aunt and uncle. I've been a negligent pretend-step-daughter.

"Ok, darling, we'll have fun."

"Yes, Mami. See you later."

"Love you, *carina*."

"Love you too."

I hang up the phone to see James standing in the doorway. He looks amused.

"Your mother is Spanish?"

"Yes. How did you know that?" I try to remember if I ever told him.

"I speak a little Spanish. I recognised the word for mummy."

"You must be good to know that *mami* is Spanish."

He shrugs. "I get by. In any case, I was hoping you might let me meet her."

"Meet my mother?"

"Yes. If you recollect, I asked you once before but it was too soon. I was hoping perhaps the events of last night…"

He moves towards the bed and sits next to me, scooping up my hand.

"Isabella," he says, staring into my eyes. "I have never felt the way about anyone that I feel about you. I would very much like to meet your family."

"What about us being seen together?" I ask. "What about photographers?"

"The ones we can't control come out at night," he says. "Paps aren't an issue during the daytime. We have budgets to keep them in hand."

"What do you mean?"

"Paps can sell the right shot for thousands," he says, "but the big money shots are always night clubs or by swimming pools. That's where the scandals happen. We pay a retainer to the worse paps to leave us alone in the daytime. They know they're unlikely to make big money for daytime shots anyway. So it works out for everyone."

"Oh."

I never realised photographers were so complicated, and make a mental note to ask Chris the next time we're doing a shoot. *If* we do another shoot, I think, remembering James's jealousy.

"In any case, they don't tend to favour busy areas," says James. "Too many normal people around and not enough scandalous activity going on."

Ok. I can see that. But do I really want him to meet my mother? She's not the most normal of people.

I take a breath. "The thing about my mother…"

"What?"

"She's… She's Spanish," I say, by way of explanation.

James laughs. "So? I've met quite a few Spanish people in my time."

I sigh, wondering how best to explain things. My parents spent part of their lives in a circus commune, and my mother's life is irregular to say the least. James Berkeley with his fancy upbringing would probably be horrified at my chaotic childhood.

"Are you embarrassed by your mother?" asks James, leaning forward in mock seriousness.

"No. It's just… She can be quite intense," I manage.

"I think you'll find me more open-minded than you think."

I pause for a moment, trying to think of another excuse.

"Where are you meeting her?" he asks.

"In Trafalgar Square. We're going to the National Gallery." This is another little quirk of my mothers. She's been to the National Gallery a hundred times, and the pictures in the main collection never change. But she loves to see it all the same. It's the artist in her, I guess.

James seems to think about this.

"Your mother likes the National Gallery?"

"She loves it."

"Would she perhaps like to see a little behind the scenes?"

"What?"

James gives me a winning smile.

"It just so happens that a close friend of mine is a curator at the museum."

"And?" I can see where this is going.

"So if you and your mother would like a tour of behind the scenes, I would be delighted to accompany you."

His face is a picture of innocence. I grin at him, slapping his arm playfully.

"James Berkeley. Are you bribing me to meet my mother?"

"Technically, I'm bribing your mother," he says, returning my grin. "But of course, I know you wouldn't be cruel enough to deny her."

He leans forward, encircling me in his arms and drawing me out of the covers.

"How long until we meet her?"

"Under an hour," I say, smiling ruefully at how he's insinuated himself into the invitation.

"That's a shame," he says, looking into my eyes. "Because it will take over an hour to do what I had planned for you."

I can tell from his expression he's not talking about breakfast. And I feel the familiar warm feeling growing again inside of me. How can he do this to me with just a few words and a look?

I blush, wondering if he knows the effect he's having.

He leans forward and kisses my forehead.

"Best I keep you nice and fresh for your Mami," he says, pronouncing the Spanish word with perfect irony. "I wouldn't like her to think I was corrupting her daughter."

"Well you are corrupting me," I say, pretending to be huffy about it.

James raises an expressive eyebrow.

"*Au contraire*, Miss Green," he says, rising to his feet with an unreadable expression on his face. "I think you'll find it is you who is corrupting me."

Chapter 21

To my delight, James suggests we walk rather than take the car to Trafalgar Square.

The morning air is refreshing, and in this part of Mayfair, there is hardly anyone on the streets. They've all either gone to work already or are waiting to descend again on St James Street at nightfall.

"I love walking London," says James.

"Don't you get mobbed by fans?" I ask, thinking people must recognise him.

He shakes his head.

"Directors are not as recognisable as you might think, Isabella. We are a little like authors in that regard. My name might be known, but my face not so much. I don't appear on screen, after all."

I call to mind of all the pictures of him and Madison at red-carpet events and think he may be under-estimating his own fame.

I've already seen a few pedestrians turn and double-take. Most directors aren't in their early thirties, tall, muscular, with sexy green eyes and ruggedly handsome features.

"I love walking in London too," I say, smiling at him because it's true. And it's nice we have something in common. With his glamorous lifestyle and aristocratic upbringing, I was beginning to think we were different in every last thing.

He smiles back.

"Not everyone understands how small it is," he says, squeezing my hand. "That's the contrast with London and LA. When I first arrived in Los Angeles, I tried walking the streets to get a feel for the place. Now I take a car or go jogging."

We pass Fortnum and Mason, with its sumptuous display of hampers and expensive goods. Then we stroll by chocolate shops and patisseries, with decadent ranges of truffles and coloured meringues decorating their windows.

James takes a sudden turn, navigating us through a hidden passage which acts as a short cut through onto Regency Street. He obviously knows the London streets even better than I do.

"Did you grow up here?" I ask. "After you moved from Mauritius?"

I thought it to be a safe question, but I can feel from the sudden tension in his hand holding mine that I'm wrong.

"No," he says. "I boarded in Scotland."

The image of him waking from his dream last night comes back to me.

It's so cold here.

"It must have been hard," I venture, "to move from somewhere hot like Mauritius to somewhere as cold as Scotland."

"Yes," he says shortly. "It was."

We walk in silence for a moment until it becomes clear he doesn't plan on sharing any more details with me. Then Trafalgar Square breaks into view, and I see my mother, waving madly near a statue of a large lion.

I make a noise somewhere between a laugh and a sigh. My mother is dressed as usual in a colourful mixture of waving scarfs and tight, floral pants. Under the medley of bright fabric she wears a purple cheese-cloth shirt. At her chest and wrists is an entire market stall's worth of Mexican silver, huge semi-precious gems, and various bulky costume jewellery.

As we near she races towards me, her heavy necklaces bouncing.

"Isabella! *Carina!*" She catches me in a warm hug, kissing each of my cheeks enthusiastically, and enveloping me in a cloud of her amber perfume.

She takes a step back, clutching my chin in her hands and considering my face intently.

"How are you? How is the script writing?"

"It's going ok, Mami. I've been doing a lot of waitressing lately."

"Ooof!" she makes a dismissive noise. Then she remembers James.

"And who is this?" she asks, glancing at him and back at me, her face a picture of delight.

To my relief, she doesn't recognise him. But then my mother is hardly an avid reader of gossip magazines or tabloid newspapers. Her chaotic house is crammed full of unread novels and poems as is it.

"I am Maria, Isabella's mother," she says, reaching out her hand to James before I can answer.

"Mrs Green," says James, shaking her hand. "My very great pleasure to make your acquaintance." His face is a picture of charm. I see my mother melt.

"Ay, Isabella," she says *sotto voice*, nudging me with her elbow. "He is a handsome one."

I wince in embarrassment, but to my great relief, James laughs.

"Mrs Green," he says "Isabella tells me you enjoy the National Gallery, and it just so happens I have a good friend in the curator there. Might you be interested in seeing some parts of the gallery which are usually screened to visitors?"

That's it for my mother. I think she might well be in love with James herself.

"I would like that very much," she says. For once, she seems almost lost for words.

"Then please allow me to escort you both," says James, offering his arm first to her, and then to me.

We walk across Trafalgar Square with my mother stunned into near silence.

She's been pestering me for years for news of any romantic liaisons. So even James's existence is enough to thrill the pants off her. But that combined with his effortless charm, handsome features, and ability to pull strings to get her backstage at the National Gallery – it's no wonder she's having difficulty taking it all in.

We walk up the large marble steps into the huge doors of the Gallery. Since it's still fairly early, the only visitors are a large school party. And they've been marshalled into a single group to the side of the entrance.

James disappears to make the arrangements with his friend, and my mother's relative silence finally explodes outwards.

"Isabella!" she says accusingly. "Why did you not say you had a boyfriend! And so handsome and charming! You know I would be thrilled, why did you not tell me?"

"It's complicated, Mami," I sigh. "I'm not even sure he is my boyfriend."

She slaps my wrist.

"Ay! Isabella. If he is not your boyfriend then you must make it so."

She peers in the direction which James vanished in.

"Such a handsome man. You mark my words, Isabella. I am a good judge of men. He is worth keeping,"

She says this with a decisive nod.

James reappears with a young woman at his side.

She looks around my age, but is dressed in the aristocratic fashion, far older than her years. She has medium-length brown hair, brushed straight down, and wears a twinset of a baby-pink cashmere sweater with a matching cardigan. Her pencil skirt inadvertently highlights long slim legs, and a set of expensive looking pearls completes the look of solid, landed wealth.

I feel a sudden wave of depression. This is the kind of girl James belongs with. Not me.

She was probably 'presented' to English society at a traditional debutante ball, aged sixteen. My sixteenth birthday was a cake with my uncle and aunty, and a few other friends in a London suburb.

"You must be Isabella? And Mrs Green?" Her accent is pure cut-glass aristocracy and her smile is warm.

She shakes each of our hands in her cool, confident grasp.

"I'm Serena. James tells me you'd like to see behind the scenes?"

My mother's eyes widen. "I would *love* to," she says. "I am big fan of the Gallery. I come here at least three times a year. The light here. The *colours*. There really is no match for this collection anywhere in the world."

My mother's passion for the National Gallery was obviously the right thing to share with Serena. Her face breaks into a broad smile, and she begins chatting excitedly about the latest vision for the Collection.

James moves in beside me and takes my arm.

"Looks like this was a good chance to win around your mother," he whispers in my ear."

I smile back.

"If that was your intention, then it's worked very well. How do you know Serena?" I try and fail to keep my tone casual.

"Oh, Isabella. Do I detect a note of jealously?"

He seems charmed and delighted.

"No," I lie, annoyed that he finds this funny. "It's just that, I'm so different to the people you must have been brought up with.

How can you even be contemplating… Us… As a couple? You must know I'd never fit in."

"Isabella, I have never seen you look out of place anywhere, and I imagine you will rise to meet the challenge of my upbringing."

His grip on my arm tightens reassuringly.

"She's a cousin," he says, "on my father's side. You really have nothing to worry about."

Another cousin. I think, remembering Ben Gracey. *I wonder how many influential cousins he has?*

Serena guides us through a private door and along a corridor into a large room.

It looks very similar to other rooms in the Gallery, with one exception. I've never seen it before, or the art on the walls. Though I can readily see the paintings are similar to those exhibited outside.

My mother's face is a picture.

"That's a Constable!" she announces, turning to Serena for confirmation. Serena nods.

"The National Gallery also acts as a vault, of sorts, for great works of art," she explains. "We can't put everything on display all at once, and some paintings are too delicate to be displayed at all."

My mother is open mouthed, staring at the paintings.

"*Esa luz. Tal belleza. Este tipo de trabajo,*" she murmurs.

Serena looks confused.

"*Such light, such beauty, such work*," translates James, surprising me with his fluency.

My mother is also impressed, and turns from where she's drinking in the art with her eyes.

"You speak Spanish?" She is, naturally, delighted.

"*Sólo hablo, un poco y mal*," says James modestly.

I translate in my head.

Only a little, and that badly.

"Do you speak to Isabella in Spanish?" asks my mother. She is preparing to launch herself into a further stratosphere of joy. All my childhood, she tried to have me speak Spanish.

"I didn't know Isabella could speak it," says James, looking at me.

"I don't," I mumble.

My mother waves her hands dismissively.

"Of course she does." She catches James's eye. "Growing up, she spoke Spanish. Then she becomes a teenager. She gets embarrassed. You know how it is. Speak English, Mami! You embarrass me with my friends!"

She laughs at the recollection. I feel myself blushing, and look to see that James seems to find this memory of my upbringing amusing.

"I can imagine that," he says, not taking his eyes from mine. Then he turns to my mother. "We have not spoken in Spanish to one another, Mrs Green. Although I knew, of course, that she won a scholarship for her Spanish dancing."

"Yes, yes," my mother's eyes light up. "My daughter was my best pupil. Have you seen her dance?"

"I haven't had the pleasure." Again his eyes are on mine, searching. Damn my mother for bringing this up.

"You must ask her to show you," insists my mother. "She really is incredible. I have never seen better. Not in Spain or anywhere. The way she dances brings tears to my eyes every time. You really would imagine her to be broken-hearted."

I can see where this is going. In a moment she'll be reeling off sad memories of my father's death and how it scarred us both.

"Enough, Mami," I interrupt quickly. "James doesn't need to hear any more childhood memories."

"As you wish," says my mother, with a wink at James. He supresses a smile, and then reverts his features to an innocent blank as I catch his eye, glowering at him.

I have to admit that James is getting on with my mother better than I could have hoped. Not everyone responds well to her effusive Spanish warmth and larger than life personality. But they seem to be the best of friends already.

Chapter 22

My mother insists that James join us for lunch, and before I know, it we're all packed into her favourite Spanish restaurant, hidden away down some steps, off Tottenham Court Road.

Inside, the cavern walls are cosy, and decorated in the warm yellows and oranges of my mother's native country. And with the English streets up above hidden from view, it's easy to forget you're not in Spain.

"Did you come here before?" my mother asks James, delighted to share her secret Spanish communities with an Englishman.

"I haven't," says James, taking in the colourful décor and Spanish staff appreciatively. "It is wonderful, Mrs Green."

The complement is enough to bring a Cheshire cat smile to my mother's face.

"Please. Call me Maria," she says, making a little playful strike of his arm. "We are practically family now," she adds, with a teasing glance at me.

I signal her with my eyes. *Mami! Enough.*

She understands the gesture and opens her eyes wide in feigned innocence.

We sit on little Andalucía-style wooden chairs, and the manager and waiting staff descend in force, chatting to Mami in Spanish and welcoming her back.

"The manager is an old friend," she explains to James as the staff depart to bring wine and appetisers. "Oh!" she stands suddenly and turns to see my Uncle Robin and Aunt Carol descending the steps into the warm cavern of the restaurant.

"Robin! Carol!" my mother rushes towards them and embraces them warmly. I wait until they approach the table and then stand to hug them both, hard. I realise how long it's been since I've seen them last, and I've missed them.

They look, as usual, like the perfect London media couple.

Robin wears his usual jeans, tongue-in-cheek arty T-shirt, and converse trainers. He used to have an unkempt mop of brown hair, but since a little bald spot appeared a year ago, he reluctantly cut it all off and now wears it short. Aunt Carol loves to tease that her Peter Pan husband has grown up into a media executive.

My aunt has immaculate blonde-highlights in her shoulder-length hair. She is dressed in knee-high boots and tight dark-blue jeans with a seventies style blouse. They're both in their forties, but look about ten years younger. Though I often think there is a touch of sadness about them from not having children of their own.

It's wonderful to see them, though I see them both do a double-take when they lay eyes on James.

At first I think this is because they haven't seen me with a boyfriend since Jerome. Then I realise they both recognise him.

How could I forget? James is famous. Perhaps not to my mother – the creative hermit. But certainly to Robin and Carol, who are firmly in the media scene. My aunt and uncle both run successful media businesses in the city. He owns a design studio and she works in marketing. It goes without saying they know exactly who James Berkeley is.

I feel a wave of uncertainly. How do you introduce someone who is already known? I see Robin and Carol pause, doubtless thinking the same.

Luckily, James fields the introductions expertly, stepping in with a firm handshake and kissing Carol on both cheeks.

The appetisers arrive in a whirl, and the table is suddenly festooned with green olives, fresh bread, and dark olive oil which my mother swears is the best in the world.

Soon, we are all eating and enjoying ourselves, and I marvel at how James gets into the swing of things. You would imagine he'd known my relatives for years, rather than having just met them.

At one point, James asks my mother aside for a private conversation, and I wonder what on earth could be going on. But it gives my aunt and uncle a chance to nestle forward and quiz me.

"So, Issy," says my uncle. "No boyfriends for years and then you find yourself a famous film director."

I laugh, not knowing what to say.

"You look great together," says Carol, nodding and smiling. "How did you meet?"

"At an audition," I say, realising I'm not yet totally prepared to answer questions about James.

"Well, he obviously likes you," says Robin. "I've never seen a man look so much in love."

I flush with pleasure, but it is dawning on me that there are so many things I haven't thought out. This has all happened so fast.

Can I really expect to have a relationship with James Berkeley?

Seeing my relatives' reactions has brought it home to me. He's a famous man. I'm a normal girl. Could that ever work?

"Good for your acting career too," adds Robin, ever career-oriented.

I begin shaking my head, but then James and my mother return. What could they have possibly been talking about? I search my mother's face for clues, but she gives nothing away.

"Issy, I have to go," says James, "I'm so sorry. I had work today which I rescheduled, but I can't put it off any longer."

I nod in understanding. I didn't expect him to come meet my mother today, let alone stay for a long lunch. I check my watch. It's already 3pm.

He makes his apologies to the rest of the table, shaking hands and kissing cheeks as he eases himself out of the tightly packed group.

"Come with me to the door," he murmurs in my ear as he bends down to kiss me lightly on the mouth.

I put down my napkin and follow him, a slightly questioning look on my face.

My mother gives me a knowing glance which I ignore.

When we're out of view of the table, just before we reach the stairs, James beckons a waiter, and requests the cheque in perfect Spanish.

"You're paying the bill?" I ask. "My uncle will be offended."

James waves away my concerns. "Your uncle will understand. It is my first meeting with your family. It is my pleasure to pay."

I decide not to argue as he picks up the tab for the entire meal and leaves a generous tip. My mother will be even more delighted with him than she already is. I wonder if Carol and Robin will fill her in on his fame, and hope they don't.

He takes my hand and guides me up the narrow staircase that leads from this underground slice of Spain to the English streets above.

"What were you and my mother talking about?" I ask, now we're comfortably out of earshot of the restaurant.

"Nothing you need to know about just yet," he says with a twinkle in his eye. He's obviously enjoying teasing me, so I decide not to give him the satisfaction of continuing to ask.

"Why did you want me to come with you to the door?" I ask.

"To say goodbye properly, of course." He smiles, sweeping me close against his body, and I breathe in the smell of him.

"I couldn't kiss you as I wanted to in front of your relatives," he adds. "It might give your aunt and uncle a heart attack."

"What about my mother," I joke weakly as he tilts my chin up so I'm looking directly into his green eyes.

"Your mother is a woman of the world," he says, and before I can answer, he catches me in a deep kiss.

I feel myself surrendering to it, letting his mouth draw me into him.

"Issy," he says, between long kisses, "you have no idea how hard it is to leave you today. All I want to do is carry you to the nearest hotel and have my way with you."

I smile through the kisses at his choice of phrase. Sometimes, he really does sound like a knight of olde.

"But that will come later," he says, kissing me more firmly now, as though steeling himself to go.

"Ok," I say as he pulls away. I feel the same way, I realise. I don't want him to leave.

"You never answered my question," he adds, looking intently at me for a moment.

"What question?" I'm looking at him in confusion.

"The most important question of all, of course," he says with a slight smile. "Will you be my leading lady?"

For a moment, I'm confused by the question, and then I realise he's talking about the movie. I let out a breath.

"I… I want to," I stare up at him. It's true. I want more than anything to work with him. To find out every little bit about him. And I loved what I read of the script.

"I'm scared I'll let you down," I admit.

His eyes widen.

"That's what you're worried about?"

"I've never acted in a movie before," I say. "I've never played a lead role before. How can you possibly have so much faith in me? What if I screw up? What if I'm terrible?"

To my amazement, he throws back his head and lets out a deep laugh.

"Oh Isabella Green," he says, "your humility is very becoming. But it is misplaced."

He plants a kiss on my forehead.

"Who is the director here? Me or you?"

"You," I mutter, wondering where this conversation is going.

"And how many actresses who have stared in my movies have been slated for bad performances?"

I scowl at him, not liking to have answers drawn from me.

"None," I admit.

"Don't scowl," he whispers, "it could become a disciplinary matter."

His hand slides to my behind, and I swallow, letting the scowl drop from my features.

"I am the director and you are my actress," he says. "My job is to guide you into your best performance. I wouldn't have cast you if I didn't know I couldn't get something incredible out of you."

He's staring at me now, as though his words have a double meaning.

"What about your working style?" I press. "You said yourself you are difficult."

"It is nothing you can't handle, I promise you that." There is a glint in his eyes. "I will have my secretary send you all the movie terms and information this afternoon. You will find out more detail about your character, who you will be cast alongside, your working hours, where you will sleep. Everything."

Where I'll sleep? Was it my imagination or did I see something flash in his expression as he said that.

James pulls me close again, and this time his hand strays to my breast. I feel my body pushing forward, closer into him.

He kisses me again, and this time he is rougher, more urgent. I know what he wants by the way his mouth moves on mine, and I can't help but respond. A sudden lust for him arcs up in me like a storm.

His fingers close on my nipple, tweaking it hard. I gasp, pushing deeper into the kiss.

I feel his other hand slide down my body. His fingers pick up the hem of my dress, working underneath between my legs.

We're standing in a narrow hallway near the entrance with no one to see or hear. But still my hand automatically grabs his wrist.

"Wait," I whisper, my voice tight with lust, "not here."

He kisses me deeply, and his hand continues to slide up under my dress, prying apart my legs. The feeling of his fingers as they glide over the skin between my upper thighs is almost too much to bear. I feel my grip on his wrist weaken. His hand is stronger, pushing further up.

"Wait," I say again, but it comes out more feebly this time. The tips of his fingers gently stoke further upwards. They slide up my inner thigh, and I feel my breath grow shorter and my body tighten as desire floods through me.

The fingers slide upwards, silky on my skin, questing towards where my warmth is growing.

Then the very edges of his fingertips flick softly over where I am wet. They move lightly, teasing me. I feel as if I'm going to explode.

The feeling of his touch is too much, too good, and I don't want him to stop. I need more. This must be what addiction feels like. My body is begging for him.

His fingers begin to circle deeper, as if he can read my thoughts.

"Tell me you'll take the role," he whispers in my ear, "tell me you'll act for me."

The tip of his finger meets my clitoris, and he strokes at me expertly. I feel the edges of my body begin to melt into his touch.

"I…"

His fingers continue to move softly against my body. The feeling is irresistible. As though every nerve ending is alive.

"Tell me you'll take the role," he repeats. Beneath my dress he continues the tantalising teasing with his hand. Then he pushes three fingers deep inside me, and I almost cry aloud with pleasure.

"Say it," he commands.

I feel his fingers begin to thrust, and now he's fucking me with his hand.

"I'll take the role," I gasp, "please James…"

In the pulsing arousal he's making inside of me, I hardly know what I'm saying.

"You have no idea how much I want to be inside you right now," he whispers. "Or how much I need to have my mouth where my fingers are now."

He continues a steady and relentless thrusting as he speaks. I fade in and out of his words, the ecstasy of his movement.

A small part of my brain tries to remind me that technically, I'm in public, even though we're hidden from view. A larger part of my all-consuming desire sweeps it to silence as James works beneath my dress, forcing deep into me.

Then I hear laughter echo up from a group of diners downstairs, and it strengthens my resolve. My grip tightens on James's forearm and I pull his hand away.

He's staring knowingly into my eyes, and as I watch, he moves his fingers to his mouth and runs them over his lips.

"Delicious," he says. "I wish you'd let me finish."

I blush deep red.

My body is still a chaos of arousal. I try to drive the feelings into check.

"You can't take that agreement as binding," I say, suddenly realising what he's just elicited from me.

"Oh, I think I can," he says. "A promise is a promise, Miss Green."

He stares at me gravely, and I laugh.

"Send me the contracts," I say, "and we'll see."

"Oh no," he's shaking his head. "You just agreed to take the part. If you go back on your word now, I'm afraid I will have to discipline you. And perhaps more strongly than you'd like."

There is a hungry look in his eyes. I realise whatever he's thinking about doing to me, he would greatly enjoy.

"I haven't agreed to anything with you," I say, trying not to imagine what might be in his mind.

Spanking? Worse?

He takes hold of both of my hands and holds them firmly, so they are pinioned against my sides.

I can feel his erection pressed against me. He must still be as turned on as I am. More, perhaps, by the feel of him. He's rock hard, and I stifle the desire to touch him.

"I'm not sure I need your permission," he says, leaning closer. "I think I might already have it."

Oh no. My body is betraying me again. How does he do this to me?

I try to keep my expression neutral, but his words are making a fire inside of me.

He lowers his voice even further and leans in close to my ear.

"I think you want to be taken in-hand, Miss Green," he says. "I can see it in your eyes. I can feel it in your body. And make no mistake, if you disobey me by going back on your word, I *will* punish you."

He draws back, so he's looking directly into my eyes.

With his hands holding mine to my sides, I feel myself trembling. Though with fear or lust, I'm not sure.

"Believe me, Isabella," he says, making every word count. "What I have in mind for you will be a lot worse than a spanking."

James releases my arms and kisses my lips, but quickly this time. I feel him fading away from me, as he's done in the past. The breaking of contact since he's worked me up to this state of arousal feels almost like physical pain.

"I will send the details," he says. His voice is stern. Authoritative. "Make sure you read them thoroughly. You are due on set in less than a week, and I want you in perfect condition. You will be expected to work hard."

I open my mouth to protest, but he places a finger over my lips.

"I will also be visiting my father's estate in a few weeks," he says, his voice gentler now. "I would like you to consider joining me."

And then, with another quick kiss, he is gone, and I am left reeling in the sweet aftershock of James Berkeley.

Chapter 23

The rest of lunch passes in a whirl, and I wonder that my relatives can't see the lust still evident on my face. Certainly, James managed to leave his mark. I'm not sure how I'll be able to pass the rest of the day without seeing him.

At one point, my phone beeps, and I examine the screen to see a message from James.

Can't stop thinking about finishing what I started in the stairwell. Call you later.

I smile at the message, and look up to see my relatives are all looking at me knowingly. I flush bright red and shove the phone back into my bag.

Carol and Robin have explained to my mother about James's Hollywood fame, and she is both shocked and excited. I can tell she's not quite sure what to make of it all. But when she leaves, she hugs me and says how happy she is.

When I finally get back to my apartment after lunch, I find a note from Lorna.

"Gone out with Ben, don't wait up!"

It's pinned to a bag of my favourite cookies, and I realise this is her way of apologising. We'd planned to stay in this evening and talk over a script she'd been critiquing for me. But this will have to wait, I guess.

I pick out a cookie – vanilla and choc-chip – and munch on it distractedly. I don't mind the cancellation, really. I'd rather Lorna went out and enjoyed herself. But with Ben Gracey? I ponder this, wondering how I feel.

Every time I see Ben, he seems to tell me some damning thing about James. Then again, he's also proved to have been telling the truth. At least about the drugs. But what about the actresses signing contracts?

I realise I haven't got a full answer out of James on this one. He assured me that I wouldn't be obliged to sign away any of my personal rights on his movie.

But that doesn't mean he's never requested it of anyone else, does it?

I resolve to ask him about it, wondering how he'll respond.

Just thinking about him makes a memory of our love-making flash back into my mind. I feel a sudden bolt of lust shudder through me, making me weak at the knees.

How does he do this to me?

My phone rings, and I try and shake away thoughts of James. I pick it up. My mother's name flashes on the display.

I click to answer.

"Hi, Mami."

"*Carina*! You will never guess what has happened?"

"What is it?" Drama from my mother can be good or bad. I grip the phone tighter.

"That gorgeous man of yours!" she trills happily.

"What do you mean?"

Is she talking about James?

"He has arranged the legal things for me, darling!"

My head is a jumble, wondering what my mother means. She fills in the silence for me.

"The apartment, darling! The service charge! James took me aside at the lunch, you remember. He asked me what needed doing. He was concerned about you, paying that full charge."

"I see." Understanding dawns. James has arranged the legal matters for my mother. I try to remember telling him about the situation with the apartment. I did, I realise, a few days ago when we first had lunch. It feels like a lifetime ago.

I feel a flare of anger. What right did he have to get involved with my financial issues without my permission? And only after a few dates and, ok admittedly, some very hot nights.

But still, that doesn't give him the right to interfere with my life.

Then again, I can't deny he has done me a real favour. I hated the legal issue hanging over my mother. And I knew she disliked it too. She never would have dealt with the service charge, and I would have been paying it forever.

So James has not only spared my mother a stressful problem, but he's also saved me my entire rent.

I turn this realisation over in my mind. If he really has dealt with the service charge, then Lorna and I are now officially rent free. She'll be more thrilled than I am.

"How did he do it?" I ask.

"Oh, it was simple in the end, darling," says my mother, confident in her own legal knowledge now it's no longer her responsibility. "It was a case of investments. Your father put aside a sum of money into the service charge of the building. The interest on it is enough to pay the annual charge. It should have been done years ago!" she adds brightly. "So simple. Just move the money into a different account, and poof!"

I smile to myself as how easy she now thinks it all to be. Only a few days ago she was terrified of consulting a lawyer.

"James had it all taken care of in a few hours," she gushes. "Such a wonderful man. You hold onto him, Isabella."

I smile wryly at this. If only she knew what he wanted to do to me.

"Ok, Mami," I say, "I gotta go. I want to call James."

"Yes, of course." My mother breathes out at the obviousness of this action. "You phone him and thank him. Thank him from me. I don't know if I ever can repay him," she adds with her usual gift for drama.

"Bye, Mami."

"Bye, *carina*."

I hang up and hold the phone for a long moment, wondering whether I should call James this second, when I'm still angry at his interference, or later when I'm seeing things more rationally.

As usual, my fiery temper wins out, and I select his contact details and press to call.

His phone goes straight through to voicemail, and I am temporarily entranced by his sexy voice telling me he can't answer. I open my mouth to leave a message, decide against it, panic, and don't manage to hang up before the voicemail clicks in for a few seconds.

Great. Now when he picks up he'll know I wimped out of leaving him a message at the last minute.

Nice work, Isabella. Sophisticated.

I toss the phone onto my bed, idly wondering where he can be with no reception. James Berkeley doesn't take the London underground, after all.

Then I notice a package has been left on the kitchen counter. It's addressed to me. Lorna must have taken delivery before she went out on her date.

I know even before I pick it up that it's the movie details which James told me about. Primarily, I can tell by the elegance of the box. But when I lift it from the counter, I see the mark of his production company stamped in red on the package.

At least this is something to kill the time before I can get through to James. Already, my annoyance at his interfering is beginning to fade away.

I take another bite of cookie and carry the package into the lounge. There I demolish the rest of it in a few mouthfuls, and seat myself on the sofa.

The package is relatively plain by James's standards, though it still comes with an understated elegance.

It's slightly larger than a shoebox and wrapped in thick brown paper, the kind that old post offices used to use, and tied with a brown ribbon rather than string. But instead of a bow, the parcel has been secured with sealing wax, stamped with the company logo.

This is a work delivery, I remind myself, thinking it looks rather corporate. The others were gifts.

I pull at the red wax seal and it splinters into three pieces. After the ribbon and paper have been dispensed with, I'm left with a large box in thick cardboard. I ease off the lid, and inside are various papers and bound booklets.

Everything looks as though it has cost a fortune to produce. I'm guessing whoever handles Berkeley's design and print services are handsomely paid.

I take out the different documents and fan them out on the coffee table, wondering what to read first.

There is a thick bound booklet titled 'Berkeley Studios', which I assume details the layout and location of the studios. And maybe the accommodation as well, if there are trailers.

Then there is a printed script, a book embossed with my character's name, which I assume is background on my role, and a cast list.

A further, serious-looking book is entitled 'rules and regulations for cast'.

The difficult Mr Berkeley strikes again, I think.

I let my eyes rest on the rulebook for a moment, and then I pick up the one with the studio title instead, and flip through it.

The first page includes a pull out map, which I open with interest. The image shows the entire complex of Berkeley's studio. It's more like a small town, I think, trying to take it all in.

The map shows a dizzying number of stages, mixed in with costume and prop workshops, technical stores and post-production suites. There's a mammoth-looking tank to film water scenes, a petrol station and even stables for coach and horses. I imagine that must be for use in historical films.

My eyes pan down to what I presume is the accommodation part of the studios. I don't see any trailers marked, but there's a fitness room and health farm listed, alongside a huge canteen and restaurant-bar, and even a nursery.

I let out a low whistle. I only took one module on set management at drama school. But it's enough to know this studio is serious luxury.

James Berkeley certainly doesn't do things by half.

I feel a surge of excitement, thinking what a fun place it will be to work. Though I have no idea how I'll avoid getting lost amongst all the studios and stages.

I flip to the next page, and the location is listed, with various instructions on how to get helicopters, coaches and limousines to access the studio park.

The whole complex is located in the English countryside, forty miles or so north-east of London.

Since I don't have a car, I am wondering whether it's even possible to access on foot when I see some text lower down.

"Private cars will be provided unless actors specifically request their own transport deliver them."

Well, that's one problem dealt with then.

The next document I pick up is the casting pages. I'm wondering who'll be acting alongside me. Berkeley's films sometimes use big names, but others have been shot entirely with unknowns. In fact, he's famous for making debut appearances into Oscar-winning performances.

I flick into the pages and let my eyes scan down.

The first name listed is mine. I feel a thrill of excitement seeing Isabella Green in black and white, by the leading role.

I never wanted to be a famous actress, but I can't deny it's a heady feeling, being almost famous.

I look down the list. The leading man's role is still blank, with *to be cast*, inked in, instead of a name.

I frown about this, and read on.

Most of the names are unfamiliar, but I see at least three that make me catch my breath.

Callum Reed. He's an incredible actor, known as much for his diversity in roles as his colourful personal life. His last film was a comedy, but before that he's won accolades for serious leads and supporting roles.

No doubt Callum feels it's time he won an Oscar, so it's a no-brainer that he's working with James.

I glance at his role. He's not a lead. But from what I've read of the script, his supporting role has plenty of depth. It's a great opportunity to show off his acting talent.

I think back to what I know of Callum. He's in his mid-forties now, but in his youth he was well-known for having problems with drugs. I feel my fingers tense around papers. James must know this. How is he comfortable casting Callum, given his own chequered past?

The next name I recognise comes with a little fission of shock. Natalie Ennis. I stare at it for a moment. Natalie is not so much famous as infamous. She's known for diva tantrums and unreasonable demands. Though some feel she has sensational acting potential.

Natalie is slated to play the prostitute I initially thought James had cast me for.

I pause for a moment, remembering something, my eyes searching the coffee table.

Lying on the far end is a copy of Lorna's *Heat Magazine*, detailing all the latest celebrity scandals.

I snatch it up.

There on the front page is Natalie. She's stumbling out of a limo looking worse for wear, and the image is spliced with another of her, shouting at her boyfriend, and flipping him the bird.

Her long dark hair is falling over her face, and her tiny child-like body is barely concealed by a mini-skirt and bra-top.

I flick to the corresponding story inside the magazine.

"Natalie Reaches Melt-Down!" screams the headline. And then, in smaller letters: "Former child-star can't cope with adult life."

I let my eyes rove over the text, reading about how Natalie has a problem with drink, unsuitable men, and, occasionally, unsuitable women.

Natalie shot to fame as a young girl, and everyone thought she'd go on to be one of the greats. But she became more famous for movie-death as she grappled with personal problems.

So this is who I'll be working with, I think, deciding to reserve judgement. English newspapers and magazines are notorious for making up scandals. Perhaps Natalie has just fallen prey to the worse side of the press. And Callum's drug past was a long time ago. He's cleaned up his act since then.

I wonder how it works on-set - whether I will be spending any time with these famous people. Or if they will simply disappear to their own luxurious quarters the minute the director shouts 'cut!'

Certainly I'd be interested to meet them.

My eyes fall on the rulebook again, and I pick it up with a sigh, realising I can't put it off any longer.

I open it and begin to scan through the terms.

Some of it I recognise as standard from drama school – theatre and movie contracts were part of the curriculum. But halfway down there is a large clause concerning drug use.

Berkeley Studios operates a zero tolerance to the use of illegal drugs.

Actors who feel they need support in this matter may contact the studios before filming. We operate extensive and highly effective rehabilitation services for those willing to accept. However, once filming has begun, any actor in breach of these conditions will have their contract instantly terminated.

I read through the rest of the contract but can't find anything particularly untoward. If anything, it's more lenient than normal studio arrangements.

Under the 'overtime' category, for example, Berkeley's studio pledges to pay extra for every twenty minutes over the standard eight-hour day. In the movie world, where actor's huge pay makes directors drive them to work around-the-clock, this is unheard of.

There is a harsh-sounding clause on punctuality, however, which gives the studio the right to make pay deductions should an actor perpetually show up late.

This seems sensible, since many big names are notorious for being late to set. Legend had it that Marilyn Monroe drove directors made with her lateness.

I think of my own problem with punctuality and decide it's not bad enough to contravene the contract.

Then I remember Berkeley promising to spank me the next time I show up late and I feel my cheeks flush.

I put down the rulebook, resolving to read it more thoroughly later, and begin to sift through the rest of the documents.

There is a menu showing daily meals, which sound absolutely incredible. The menu also details other food arrangements laid on. There's an extra crew of trained chefs to provide for vegans and other special diets. Generally, actors in Berkeley's studio can more or less have anything they'd like made fresh to order.

Then there are details on the accommodation. It looks as though we won't be in trailers after all. The extra buildings which I'd mistaken for studios are, in fact, little stand-alone lodges. One for each actor.

There's a picture of the interior, and inside the lodges are hotel-style suites, complete with their own kitchen and lounge areas.

On the list of amenities are luxuries I'd never even heard of, including 'make-up fridge' and 'automatic water-filter faucets'.

Maybe this is what it takes to keep modern movie divas happy. But something tells me this is just Berkeley's way of doing everything perfectly.

My phone rings, and I snatch it up, smiling to see James's name on the display.

"Are you angry with me?" he says, his deep voice echoing richly down the line.

"No. Yes…" I stutter over the words, realising I'm no longer angry. And he doesn't sound the least bit sorry anyway.

"Well, what is it? Yes or no?" Now he sounds amused.

"Yes," I decide, electing to be annoyed on principle, even though I'm not really feeling it anymore. "You shouldn't have interfered in my personal financial affairs without asking me."

"I plan to interfere with a great deal more than your personal finances."

The way he says the words makes me melt, and I inwardly curse him for having this effect on me.

"It was impolite," I insist, trying to collect myself.

"Well now," he says, "the last thing I would ever want is to be discourteous. Especially to you. Did you get the movie documents?"

"Yes. Don't change the subject."

"I have some unfortunate news, Isabella." His voice sounds stern, and I feel my stomach turn to ice. My first thought is I'm no longer in the movie.

"I've got to go away for a week," he says, and I feel my breathing steady.

"Oh," I say with relief. And then the reality hits me. A week without James Berkeley. That seems like forever.

"An urgent matter has come up," he adds, "we'll talk about it on my return. I'm not sure how good the phone reception is where I'll be."

Oh. A little part of my heart whimpers. *Where could he be going with no reception?*

All kinds of paranoid thoughts flood my brain. When a man tells you he's headed somewhere and he can't talk on the phone, it can't be good.

Is he breaking up with me?

"Can't we talk about it now?" I ask in a small voice.

"No, Issy." He sounds angry. Then his voice softens. "This is nothing to do with how I feel about you. That hasn't changed. It's just something unexpected that has come up. I won't know what it means for the movie until I get back."

Oh. So something to do with the movie. Selfishly, I hear myself worrying that the picture will be canned.

Listen to you, I scold myself. *A week ago, you never even wanted to be in a movie.*

"Are you OK?" I say, worrying now that he might be in some personal trouble.

"I am absolutely fine," he says. "You never need to worry about me. But the state you got me worked up unto earlier today...." I hear the promise in his voice. "Perhaps you need to worry about what I might do to you when I get back."

I feel myself smiling, but I'm still not reassured. "When do you leave?" I ask.

"Right now. I'm at the airport. I had to bribe security to let me out to call you," he adds.

Is he telling the truth?

"Listen, Issy I have to go," says James. "I... I'll talk to you when I get back."

And then he's gone.

I stand for a long moment with the phone in my hand. All the events of the past few days rush through my mind in a blur.

The tango, the hotel, his meeting my family. And now this phone-call. I feel a slow sense of foreboding sweep through me.

After all this, was that phone-call a way of letting me down gently?

I shake away the thought as ridiculous. But other, logical facts begin assailing my mind.

You've known him less than a week. You didn't exactly play hard to get. He said himself he's troubled and difficult.

James said on the phone that his feelings hadn't changed. But he also said he's going somewhere with no mobile reception for a week. And he's given me no reason for why that could be.

A deep painful feeling seeps into me. I have a very long week ahead.

Somehow I must get through the next seven days without James Berkeley.

Seven days, without knowing why he's gone.

It feels like forever.

And there is nothing I can do but wait.

I hate that they left me hanging!

Don't worry! If you enjoyed *Close-Up and Personal*, the next book in the series, *The Berkeley Method* is out now, and available to buy on Amazon for $2.99.

Shhh! Want a secret scene from James Berkeley's past that not even Isabella knows?

Go to: *http://eepurl.com/w45Rf*

You'll also be given access to reader resources, with pictures of locations, toys, and underwear featured in the series.

AND

Dates of SECRET SALES where you can bag the next Spotlight release for only $0.99c!

A personal word from JS Taylor:

"Thanks so much for reading my book. Fun books can make a bad day better. So if you enjoyed my writing, it would mean the world to me if you post your thoughts on Amazon review. Many Kindles give the option to do this on the next page. If you really want to make my day, you can even share what you're reading with friends on Facebook and Twitter.

I read every review, and often test free copies of future books on readers who like my work."

"I also take every kind of reader feedback very seriously, so if you have a critique, or something you didn't like, please let me know. This means I can become a better writer for my readers. Contact me at: jstaylor@pageturners.uk.com."

ABOUT JS TAYLOR

Jennifer Sarah Taylor won her first story-writing competition aged eight and has never looked back. In adult life she discovered it was much easier to make men do what she wanted in fiction than in the real-world. So she's been forcing her male characters to make romantic gestures ever since. As an avid Fifty Shades fan, she was delighted to discover the world was ready for hotter love-scenes. She humbly hopes her readers enjoy reading the Spotlight Series as much as she loved writing it.

DON'T FORGET TO SHARE YOUR THOUGHTS ON CLOSE UP AND PERSONAL...

Not sure how to write a review? It's easy!

Three steps to the perfect Amazon book review...

1. Say what you liked about the book.
2. Explain which kind of readers might enjoy it.
3. State any other books the title is similar to.

85

CPSIA information can be obtained at www.ICGtesting.com
Printed in the USA
BVOW021132140713

325897BV00012B/422/P